Till Death Do Us Pot

A Flower Shop Mystery
Fall Novella

Kate Collins

TILL DEATH DO US POT
A Flower Shop Mystery Fall Novella

ISBN: 9798560778668

Cover design by Arash Jahani

CONTENTS

DEDICATION

To my children, Jason and Julia – my support, my encouragers, my beacons of light. I truly could not do this without you. This book is also dedicated to all of you who love Abby, Marco, and the gang at Bloomers who make up the heart and soul of The Flower Shop Mysteries.

PROLOGUE

ABBY KNIGHT SALVARE

Monday, November 12th
5:45 p.m.

"Tell me a little about yourself, Abby."

I appraised the man sitting across from us in an overstuffed armchair. He was a big man with thinning brown hair, an oval face, dark eyes, and a long chin. He had a notepad in his lap and a pen in his left hand. A leftie.

"I'm a florist. I own a flower shop called Bloomers on the town square right here in New Chapel. You may have heard of it. I also have a cute little, three-legged rescue dog and a beautiful Russian Blue cat."

He wrote it down. "Interesting that you felt it important to mention that your dog has three legs."

I stared at him.

He turned to my husband, sitting beside me on a beige tweed sofa. "And Marco, tell me about you."

"I own Down the Hatch Bar and Grill, also on the town square. I'm a former Army Ranger."

The marriage counselor gave a little smile and wrote it down. "Being a former Army Ranger is important to you, isn't it?"

Marco glanced at me as if to say, *Is this guy for real?* Then he answered, "just part of my bio."

"I see. Abby, what do you see as the strengths in your relationship with Marco?"

I looked at my sexy hubby, with his dark hair that drooped casually onto his forehead and curled at the back of his neck, his soulful brown eyes, his square jaw, his expressive mouth, his broad shoulders . . .

I shook myself out of my reverie and focused. "Well, we love each other. That's a strength. We trust each other. We're there for each other. We have many of the same likes . . ." I paused.

"Okay," the counselor said. "And you, Marco?"

Marco gazed into my eyes, a smile curving his mouth at the corners. "Ditto."

"Could you express your feelings?"

"I feel the same way Abby does."

That was my husband, a man of few words. A man of action, integrity. A man I loved with all my heart.

The counselor looked from me to Marco. "So, what brings you two here today?"

I started. "We're having problems communicating. I feel like I'm not heard when I speak to him."

"Marco, is that a fair statement?"

Marco rubbed his chin. "I don't know about fair. Maybe I've been a little short lately."

"And why are you being short with your wife?"

Marco glanced at me again. "I think sometimes she may be a little too impulsive. It's hard to communicate that without hurting her feelings."

"I'm impulsive?"

Marco squeezed my hand. "I'm sorry, babe. Adorably impulsive. But sometimes I worry about you."

I squeezed back, harder than he had. "What do you worry about, sweetheart?"

"I worry that you'll get yourself into a situation and I won't be able to help you."

"I don't always need your help," I said.

Marco tried to hide his smile. "Disregard my comment," he said and squeezed my hand again. "Let's move on to more important topics."

I pulled my hand away. "Says someone who's a *little* too controlling."

Marco looked at me in surprise. "Too controlling?"

I gave him a tight smile. "As I said, a little."

"In what way?" the counselor asked.

They were both watching me now, waiting for my answer. "You like to schedule every minute of the day. Sometimes I just like to kick back and relax."

"You know I have to do that because –" Marco caught himself. "You're right. I do schedule things. I'll have to work on that."

"Let's go over some tools for you to use, Marco. We can start with –" The counselor glanced at the clock on the wall, stopping mid-sentence. He seemed to shift uncomfortably in his chair before standing and walking to his desk. "We'll have to end it there for today."

CHAPTER ONE

TARA KNIGHT

Sunday
Six days earlier

Was there anything worse than a Sunday night during the school year? I didn't think so. All of the excitement from the weekend had faded by then, replaced by the creeping dread of unfinished homework assignments, research paper due dates, and history exams, not to mention the social anxiety and mental torture of trying to fit in with the fickle, fabricated, fuss of hormonal teenagers.

And history exams.

Don't get me wrong. I loved Monday mornings. Starting the week refreshed and energized, ready to take on whatever New Chapel High School dared throw in my direction filled me with a buzz of electricity, and especially now that I'd finally had an opportunity to work on the project of my dreams, I was more excited than ever. I looked down at the assignment for journalism class. Write a fictional investigative journalism piece. Awesome.

My mom stepped into my room. "Do you need help studying?"

My shoulders slumped. I pushed aside the journalism assignment and pulled the history book from my backpack. I hadn't looked at the book all weekend and the test was in five days.

Did I mention how much I hated history exams?

"No, Mom," I said solemnly.

"Dinner will be ready soon," she said. "Wash up and come downstairs."

"Coming," I replied, but suddenly my focus was averted by a distant, blood-curdling scream from outside. My little dog Seedling popped up from a deep sleep and his ears perked up. I leaned over my desk to look out the window. Way off to my right I could see a group of kids playing tag in their backyard.

My desk sat in front of my second-floor bedroom window. From there I could see the backyards of our next-door neighbors, as well as the backyards of our neighbors on the next street. To my immediate right was a large oak tree where a thick limb held a long swing with a wooden seat. To my left was a yard with a green turtle sandbox where young kids sat on hot summer days building sandcastles with little plastic shovels. To the far right, I could still see the group of children playing flashlight tag in the growing darkness, wearing hoodies and jackets on this cool autumn evening.

To my far left, I caught another sight, a tall boy with short brown hair wearing a green and white varsity jacket, raking leaves into little piles. There was a glare on my window, so I leaned further over the desk and turned my lamp off. There he was. The only reason I had ever, and would ever, look forward to a history class.

From downstairs I heard, "Tara, dinner is on the table."

"Okay, Mom," I called. "I'll be right down."

I was Tara Abigail Knight, middle-named after my aunt Abby, the owner of Bloomers Flower Shop and one of my personal heroes. Twelve years younger than her, I was a junior in high school and was just as feisty and bold as my aunt, or so I've been told. I also took after Aunt Abby in looks, inheriting her fiery red hair, petite frame, and zest for anything that smelled of mystery.

What I should also mention was the reason why I didn't mind history class all that much. The reason's name was David Harrison, a dark-haired, blue-eyed football player who lived in the house kitty-cornered across the backyard from my house. His bedroom also faced the back and he often left the curtains open while he studied . . . not that I would know. And he sat two seats behind me in third-period history class.

David and I had been friends in middle school, mostly due to our houses' proximity. It seemed as though just a few years ago we'd been the kids outside playing flashlight tag, running through piles of leaves and having fun. But all of that had changed in high school when David became the popular kid and I just became the girl next door – or across the back yard. We still talked and joked in class, but I knew not to get my hopes up. What chance did I have with a football player?

Something red caught my eye, drawing my attention to the house directly opposite mine, way across my yard and the neighbors' yard, where I saw a girl through her window wearing a bright red top of some kind. The girl was my age and was in my homeroom. Deena something. She and her family had just moved into the house over the summer and I really hadn't had a chance to get to know her, or, more honestly, I hadn't taken the chance.

Even though it was getting dark outside and the lights were on in her room, I couldn't see much. The house was too far away. But something seemed odd. The way she paced in front of her window, stopping momentarily to look outside, seemed strange.

Allen. That was it. Deena Allen.

"Tara, now!"

"Coming, Dad."

My dad, Jordan Knight, was Aunt Abby's older brother. He had red hair, too, just not as bright red. He also had that quick Irish temper that all of the Knights inherited. When he started calling my name, I knew I was pushing my luck. I dropped my history book back into my schoolbag and rushed downstairs for dinner.

✿❀✿

Sometime during the night, I was dreaming about David winning a football game and presenting me with his varsity jacket as a symbol of his undying devotion when the jacket fell on the ground at my feet with a heavy thud. I awoke with a start and lay there for a moment wondering what had awakened me. Seedling jumped up and placed his paws on the side of my bed. I leaned over to scratch his ear. "Go to sleep, puppy."

My little puppy, Seedling was no longer a puppy, but he still had the scrunched-up face and fuzzy ears that were too large for his head. His fur was a mixture of muted greys and browns, and his breed couldn't even be identified by our vet, but I refused to call Seedling a mutt, even though that's how they'd described his mother, Seedy, when Abby had rescued her. Thankfully, my mom and dad had let me take in the little guy, saving his life, and allowing me a furry best friend.

I had just turned on my side and closed my eyes when I heard a creaking sound coming from somewhere far outside my window. I glanced at the clock. Three a.m.

Because I was now wide awake, I lay there pondering the source of that noise. A tight window frame? A door that needed greasing? Surely it wasn't David trying to get my attention.

Okay, now you're just fantasizing.

I had left my window open just a crack because my parents like to sleep in a sauna, but as I tried to fall back asleep, I felt an icy breeze blowing into the room. I climbed out of my warm bed and leaned over my desk, parting the curtain to look across the yards to David's window. His curtains were drawn, and his light was out. In fact, all of the lights across the yard from mine were out, except for one.

Deena Allen's house had a back door off the garage with a small outdoor light glowing softly above the frame. I caught movement in the dark yard as my eyes adjusted. A tall dark figure was dragging something long and bulky and soft from the garage. He appeared to be heading toward the shed at the far back of his lawn, a shed that abutted our yard. I could just make out the edge of the shed's door, which meant it was standing open, no doubt where the creaking sound had come from.

What was he doing out there at three a.m.?

I felt a chill crawl up my spine. What indeed? I crept past my parents' room, moved quickly down the stairs to the den, grabbed the binoculars my mom used to watch birds, and tip-toed back upstairs, where I stood at the window with the binoculars pressed to my eyes and the curtain draped over one shoulder. Up close, I could see that the figure was a large man, probably Deena's father. He was dragging a long, thick object wrapped in some kind of material into the shed. At that point, I lost him from sight.

I waited at least five minutes until he came out, brushed his hands together, shut the shed door, and glanced all around. I shifted position and he looked up. I quickly stepped back, letting the curtain drop, my heart racing. Had he seen me spying on him? A minute later I heard the creaking sound again. I peered through the crack between the curtains and the backyard was empty. The backyard light was off.

I quietly closed the window and joined Seedling who was now curled up by my pillow. I lay still and pet him, now wide awake.

What had I just witnessed?

CHAPTER TWO

ABBY

Monday

Monday mornings at Bloomers always started with a hearty breakfast, a good way to leap into a busy work week. This morning when I got to the shop, my assistant Grace was in the coffee and tea parlor brewing coffee, Lottie, my other assistant, was no doubt at the computer in the workroom viewing the new orders, and I could hear Rosa, the latest addition to our design team, singing in the kitchen at the back of the shop as she prepared her now-famous *Huevos Marisol*, a delightful Columbian egg dish that already had my mouth watering.

"Abby, love," Grace said, coming toward me carrying a cup of her delicious brew, "I've got the donation bin set up in the parlor, but I'm afraid it's taking up too much space."

"It would get more attention out here, Grace. I can take the display of mums to the register and you can move the donation box next to the front door. There's plenty of room."

"Then move it I shall."

As usual, the sixty-something widow was sporting a skirt and sweater set, her short silver hair accenting her oval face and fine English features. She had come to me with an idea to help our local women's shelter where she volunteered on Saturdays. We would collect gently used clothing and Grace would take it to the shelter. She'd told us that many women had to vacate their homes quickly in their need to get away from abusive spouses and often had to leave everything they owned behind. Our donations would be very welcome. I'd agreed to the plan immediately. It was a great way to give back to the community.

I took a sip of Grace's fragrant brew and glanced around my shop as I walked toward the curtain. The three-story red brick building that housed Bloomers dated back to about 1900 and still had original tin ceilings, brick walls, and wood floors. There were two big bay windows, one in the shop and one in the coffee and tea parlor, with the yellow frame door in between.

Near the door was a cashier's counter; in the middle of the room was a round oak table used to hold floral arrangements; on one wall was an antique armoire used for display purposes; and along the rear wall was a glass display case for fresh flowers, a charming wicker settee, and a tall dieffenbachia plant in the corner. Around the perimeter were potted green plants of all sizes just waiting for new homes.

"Breakfast is served," Lottie called from the kitchen.

I parted the purple curtain and stepped into my paradise, the workroom, where the magic happened. I stowed my purse in the bottom desk drawer, put my jacket over the back of my chair, tied on my yellow bib apron, and glanced around.

My desk was part of a laminate counter that ran around the room, with open shelves above for floral containers of all sizes, shapes, and materials. Below the counter were drawers and cabinets for more storage. A large, slate-topped worktable sat in the center, with drawers for my florist tools beneath it.

On the opposite wall stood two gigantic walk-in coolers. Made of stainless steel, with thick, insulated doors, cooler number one stored all of our stock, while number two stored the arrangements waiting to be delivered.

I walked into the kitchen and found Rosa serving up her eggs onto four plates. "*Vamos!* Get them while they are hot," she called.

Lottie came into the kitchen behind me, with Grace last in line. We heaped on the eggs, grabbed pieces of toast, and took our plates out to the parlor where we sat at a white wrought iron table and discussed plans for the day.

I had a great crew. Lottie Dombowski, a big woman with brassy curls and a fondness for the color pink, was the original owner of Bloomers. I'd worked for her during my college breaks, loving every minute of it. Then, after being booted out of law school and feeling down on my luck, I'd looked around to see what I wanted to do with my life, thought of Bloomers, and headed back to where I'd been happiest, only to discover that Lottie was selling the business. Her husband Herman had undergone heart surgery and they were so deep in debt from the staggering amount of medical bills that she had been forced to sell.

So I'd scraped up the rest of the college fund my grandfather had left me, put a down payment on the happy little flower shop, and had myself an instant career. Lottie had taken me under her wing and taught me everything she knew, and now we worked together as a team.

The next member we'd added to that team was Grace Bingham, a naturalized citizen from Great Britain who'd had many occupations before joining Bloomer's staff. Now she ran the coffee and tea parlor, serving up gourmet coffee, a multitude of teas, and her homemade scones, a different flavor every day.

Our last member was Rosa Marisol Katarina Marin, a gorgeous, dark-haired, Columbian native with a gift for creating beautiful floral arrangements. Rosa had hired Marco and me to find out who'd killed her husband and had become so eager to help us during a particularly busy time, we'd ended up hiring her.

I had just taken my last bite when my cell phone rang. I pulled it out of the apron pocket and saw my cousin's name on the screen. "Hi, Jillian."

"Abs, I'm on my way over. You have to see the new outfit I bought Harper for the holidays."

"Okay. Just knock on the –"

I heard a knock.

I rose from the table, walked out of the parlor, and saw Jillian standing at the door with the baby carriage.

Jillian Knight Osborne was my first cousin and the exact opposite of me in temperament. She was a head taller, a year younger, and ten pounds lighter. Her hair was also several shades lighter than my fiery red bob. She had a husband named Claymore and a one-year-old baby girl named Harper, an adorable, sweet-natured child who was the apple of her eye. And because Jillian was a fashionista and a personal shopper, Harper gave her someone else to focus her design attention on.

"You have to see this," Jillian said as she wheeled the carriage into the shop. She pulled back the blanket and there was Harper dressed in a bright orange dress with brown fur trim, brown leggings, orange shoes with curled up toes, and an orange bonnet trimmed with brown fur.

"Look!" she said, holding the child up. "My little pumpkin!"

I had to admit Harper looked adorable. Lottie, Grace, and Rosa came out of the parlor and began cooing over her.

"Let me get a picture of her," Rosa said, and scurried away to get her cell phone.

"May I?" Grace asked, and at Jillian's fervent nod, she picked Harper up and cradled her in her arms. "Lovey, you take first prize for the most adorable pumpkin ever."

"Okay, everybody," Rosa called. "Stand next to Harper."

With Grace still holding her, we all gathered around and smiled. After several photos, Grace handed Harper back to Jillian, who slipped her back into her stroller. "That's all I wanted," she said. "We were out for a stroll, so I thought I'd stop by. Oh, what's this for?"

"That's a donation bin," Grace said. "We're collecting gently used clothing for the women's shelter. If you have clothes to donate, we'd be more than happy to take them."

"*If* I have clothes?" Jillian laughed. "The question actually is, can I part with my clothes."

"Oh, come on, Jill," I said. "There must be things in your closet that you no longer wear."

Jillian tapped her chin. "I'll have to go home and look. And don't raise your eyebrows at me, Abby Knight. I'm sure I'll find something."

"It's Abby Knight *Salvare,* Jill."

She wrinkled her nose. "You'll always be Abby Knight to me."

Lottie checked her watch. "Okay, everyone. Ten minutes until we open. Are we set?"

"I'll let you get back to work," Jillian said. "The nanny will be coming over soon. I have a client coming in at ten o'clock."

"Find some clothes to donate," I called as she wheeled the carriage out of Bloomers.

As the door shut, the store's phone rang, the computer dinged with incoming orders, and so the day began.

By three o'clock we had completed eighteen orders, made four deliveries, and were still working. At three-thirty, Lottie pushed her brassy curls away from her forehead with the back of her hand and let out a breath. "I need a break."

She'd barely gotten the words out of her mouth when Grace came through the purple curtain bearing a tea tray on which sat a teapot, a stack of cups and saucers, several packets of sugar, and creamer.

"Teatime," she called and set the tray down on the worktable.

I straightened and glanced around at the clock on the wall. "It's Monday, ladies, and it's nearly three-thirty."

Everyone knew what that meant. My mother, Maureen Knight, or "Mad Mo," as her family affectionately called her, always came in on Mondays with her latest creative endeavor. She taught kindergarten during the week but on weekends she was a wannabe artist. She'd created many pieces over the years I'd owned Bloomers, such as her infamous footstool, made with authentic-looking bare feet, her children's bat mobile, made with hanging bats, her palm tree coat rack, with hooks made to look like outstretched hands, and her tea cart, made with golf clubs and tees. She brought them to Bloomers for me to sell, thinking the profits would help my shop.

My mother had good intentions, but many of her art pieces were just too weird to sell. Those we ended up stashing in the basement, never, ever mentioning it to her.

"I can't wait to see what she has for us today," Grace said.

Lottie just rolled her eyes.

Five minutes later, the purple curtain parted, and my mom peeked in. "Guess who?"

I gave her a kiss on the cheek, and she slid onto a wooden stool at the worktable, parking a brown cardboard box next to her. "Grace told me about your donation bin. I'm going home right away to see what all I can give."

"Thanks, Mom."

"In the meantime, I have to show you my new art project." She leaned over to grab the box and pulled out a glass canning jar filled with red wax and a white wick sticking out of the top. She handed it to me. "What does this smell like to you?"

I took a whiff. My stomach lurched and I pulled the candle quickly from my nose. I held a smile firmly in place as I tried to deduce the smell she'd intended. "Smells like pizza."

"This is my Italian spice candle." She pulled out a glass jar filled with black wax and handed it over.

I held the candle just a bit further away and breathed mostly through my mouth. "Soy sauce?"

"Japanese Cuisine."

"I sense a theme," Grace said as she approached. She was handed the next candle, colored bright yellow. I watched her take a deep breath and was surprised by the smile that swept across her face. "Smells like sweet corn on the cob."

"Right on the nose, Grace. They're dinner candles. Unlike the traditional, boring dinner candles, these actually smell like dinner. Take the Italian spice for instance. Burn it when you're having Italian food, and everyone enjoys the meal even more."

"How much are you asking for them?" Rosa asked.

"I thought nine ninety-five would do it."

I was surprised by the honest reactions of my staff. A candle that smelled like Italian food was the last thing in the world I would want to light in my house, but I had to admit the idea was intriguing. And for less than ten bucks, it was an idea that just might sell.

"I thought we could set them out on the big round table," Mom said. "Now that the chilly weather is here, it's just right for candle season."

I smiled at her. "Let's do it."

Her eyes sparkled with excitement as she hopped off the stool, repacked her cardboard box, and took it to the sales floor, where she began setting out the candles. When she'd finished, there were eight candles on the table.

Rosa looked at each of them and picked up a dark yellow candle. "This smells like tacos. Abby, smell."

This time I inhaled deeply and felt a mild rumble of hunger in my belly. It really did smell like Mexican food.

Rosa held the candle back up to her nose and smiled. "I'd like to buy the Mexican Fiesta, Maureen."

"Abigail," my mom said, always calling me by my full name, "ring her up."

"I'll be right back with the money," Rosa called and darted through the curtain.

My mom gave me a hug. "Thank you, honey. I'm so glad you like them."

An older couple came into the shop and walked up to the checkout counter for assistance, so Mom said her goodbyes and left.

"May I help you?" I asked.

"We hope so," the woman said. "We have to attend an anniversary dinner this evening. Do you have something readymade that we can take?"

"We do. Let me show you what we have in our display case."

The woman started to follow me, then stopped to see the candles. "Italian Spice," she read off. "Down Home Cooking, Mexican Fiesta . . . Look at these, Sam. Wouldn't one of these be nice to take, too?" She glanced up at me. "Which one is your best-seller?"

"We just got those in, so I'm not sure what we have."

"Oh, look. Here's one that says New Delhi Curry. That should be perfect."

My mom had just made her first sale.

Thirty minutes later my phone rang, and Marco's name appeared on the screen. "Hey, what's up?" I asked.

"Hello, beautiful. Got any dinner plans?"

"Not really, but suddenly I'm in the mood for tacos."

"Okay, just checking to see if you wanted me to bring something home from the bar. And hey, guess what? We've got a new client."

"That's great! What's the case?"

"A woman wants us to locate her missing twin brother. I'm going to see her right now. We can discuss the particulars over dinner."

"Okay. I'll have the salad ready and the wine poured."

"It's a date, Sunshine."

I hung up with a smile. Marco wasn't just my husband, he was also my best friend, my hero. We'd met just after I'd bought Bloomers when my beloved vintage Corvette had been hit out front by a hit-and-run driver who had ended up being a suspect in a murder case. Marco had come down the street from his bar, Down the Hatch, to see what the ruckus was about and had ended up helping me solve the case. We'd been a twosome ever since. We'd gotten married just under a year ago, and now we had a house and two pets.

I was living the dream.

TARA

After school, I watched the house across the yard while I sat at my desk pondering the story I had to write for my journalism class. The assignment was to write a news article that would hook the reader's attention immediately, and it was due the next day. Instead of writing it, however, I pulled the binoculars from under my desk and watched the bedroom opposite mine, where Deena, now in a blue top, was curled up on her bed reading. I watched as a younger girl came in a sat at the foot of the bed, pulled her knees up, and wrapped her arms around them. They talked for a moment, then Deena scooted to the edge of the bed to hug her.

In the yard next to hers, David appeared, wearing a gray hooded sweatshirt and blue jeans. I followed him with my magnified gaze as he began to rake the leaves that had fallen around a big elm tree in his back yard, adding to the pile he'd made a few days before. I sighed with longing.

David had actually talked to me in history class that morning, asking me how much I'd studied for the upcoming test. I'd joked that I hadn't even started. He'd laughed and said the same. I should have asked him if he wanted to study together, but as always, my mind had gone blank. I watched as David stopped raking, wiped his forehead with his sleeve, and disappeared around the side of his house. *Come on, tree. Drop more leaves.*

A moment later movement in Deena's window caught my eye and I glanced over to see a large figure standing in Deena's doorway. I watched as the man whom I assumed was her father talked to her. She scooted to the edge of her bed, got up, and slammed the door in his face. Wow. My dad would've taken the door down if I'd slammed it in his face, but I scanned the windows and saw her father appear in the living room a few moments later. He sat down in the dim glow of a television screen. I looked back up to see Deena give her sister another long hug.

What a sweet sight. Made me wish I had a sister. Or a brother.

Yes, I'd take a brother, too.

I watched for another five minutes, then closed the curtains and sat back in my chair, still contemplating the scene across from me. In reality, If I would've been angry enough to slam the door in my father's face, my mom would've been right up to find out why, which made me wonder where Deena's mom was.

I'd seen her mother in the backyard over the summer, working in a garden on the left side of their shed. Deena and her younger sister would often come out to help her pick weeds. In fact, I had remembered seeing Deena's mother way more often than her father. So where was her mother now?

I didn't like the feeling I was getting, that something was wrong over there. Maybe the parents had divorced. But would the mother really leave the girls behind? I stuck my chin on my palm with a sigh. I hated mysteries I couldn't solve.

Around six o'clock, a light came on in David's room. I looked down at the binoculars standing upright on my desk. Was I really going to start spying on my neighbors? He was leaning toward the window, hands braced on his desk, looking out on the scene below. Several kids with flashlights ran by and trampled through the piles of leaves. I chuckled to myself, then sat down and bent my head over my book, just in case he glanced my way. Discreetly checking, I could see him staring down as the kids left the yard, laughing and chasing each other. If only I could think of a way to attract his attention like that.

The feature article, Tara. I picked up my pen and began to write about a girl who lived across the yard, a girl who appeared to have no mother and who wouldn't talk to her father, a man who had dragged something mysterious out of the house and into a shed in the middle of the night. A man who had secrets. A man with a missing wife.

I was going to ace this assignment.

CHAPTER THREE

ABBY

A little after six o'clock that evening I stepped from the attached garage into our cute little ranch house and was greeted by Seedy, our three-legged rescue dog, whose plumy tail was wagging excitedly. She was joined by Smoke, our Russian Blue cat, who wound around my legs, nearly tripping me as I walked into the kitchen.

Marco was standing at the kitchen island, pouring wine into two glasses.

I put my purse down and accepted a glass. "You're home early."

"We have to eat a quick dinner," Marco said. "Our case starts tonight."

"Then here's to a new client," I said, and he clinked glasses with me. Because our PI business was relatively new, we were always happy to have a new client.

"To Team Salvare," Marco added.

I took a sip and set the glass aside so I could heat up the food Marco had brought home. "Tell me about the case."

Marco sat on a stool at the kitchen island. "A woman named Sylvie Freeman called me this afternoon about her missing brother. She was practically hysterical over the phone, so I went to see her. She reported that her twin brother, Frank Vesco, hasn't called her in a week and she can't reach him. She tried to phone Frank while I was there, but he didn't answer."

"A missing person's case?"

"Possibly," Marco said. "I asked Sylvie to call Frank's wife, Eileen Vesco, who claims that Frank is on a fishing trip."

"Okay, not a missing person's case."

"But after she got off the phone with Eileen, Sylvie said that her brother would have mentioned the trip to her. She said he shares everything with her. So, we have conflicting stories."

"Frank's wife wasn't worried?"

"Not at all. Eileen Vesco seemed annoyed by Sylvie's questions." Marco set the glass down and swirled the red liquid along the sides of the glass. "Then Sylvie called Frank's best friend and fishing buddy, saying if anyone would know about the trip, it would be him. And he had no idea that Frank had gone away."

"Seems like the wife is lying."

Marco nodded. "That's exactly what Sylvie said."

I took a sip of wine, thinking it over. "Where are we going to start?"

"We'll start with Frank's best friend, a man by the name of John Thompson."

"What about Frank's wife?" I asked. "Shouldn't we start with her?"

"Usually, we would, but I don't think she's going to be very helpful until we can dig up some more information. Hopefully, John can give us a little unbiased insight. I've already set up an appointment to meet with him tonight, right after dinner."

"Then let's eat dinner and get this investigation started."

Marco reached his arms around my waist and rested his chin on my shoulder, kissing me lightly on the cheek. "I love you, Sunshine."

"Come in," John Thompson said with a smile. "Please."

He was a tall, gangly man with brown hair, a receding hairline, and a plump face, wearing jeans and a pullover sweater. He led the way into a cozy living room where a fire crackled in the fireplace and a mounted trophy of a fish hung over the mantle. On the wall were art prints with a fishing theme, pictures that would've looked right at home in Marco's bar.

A thin, pleasant-looking woman stood up from her recliner and smiled at us.

"Sally, this is Marco Salvare," John said, "and his wife Abby."

She extended her hand to me. "I'm so glad you contacted us. John has been worried about Frank ever since his sister called us."

"Have a seat," John said, offering the brown plaid sofa.

We sat down and I took out the notebook and pen.

"As I told you on the phone," Marco began, "we'd like to get some background information on Frank."

"What do you need to know?"

Marco took the lead. "How long have you known Frank?"

"Well," John said, "I'd have to go back to our college days, thirty years or so."

"Then you know him well."

"He's been like a brother to me."

"And how often do you go on fishing trips together?"

John shrugged. "I don't know. A few times a year."

Sally looked at him askance. "Make that ten times a year, John."

"Nah, not anymore," he replied. "We used to go on several big trips every year up to Michigan or Canada, but as we've gotten older, we're more inclined to stay local. I'd say every few months we'll try to get away. But it's been at least three months since we've been out roughing it in the wild. That's why I was surprised to hear he'd gone on a fishing trip without me."

I wrote it down.

"Is it like Frank to cut off all communication with his family?" Marco asked.

"I wouldn't say all communication. Frank always called his wife to let her know we'd arrived."

"What about his sister?" Marco asked. "Would he have called her?"

John smiled at the thought. "I'd almost forgotten about Sylvie. He most definitely would've called her. There are severe repercussions for upsetting Frank's sister." He laughed. "She's a sweet lady, but she's got a few screws loose."

Sally gave her husband a playful swat. "Jonathan."

He winked at her and continued. "There was this one time when Frank shut off his phone for the week. He was tired of Eileen nagging him and Sylvie checking up on him, so he put his phone in the bottom of his suitcase and left it in the cabin. Three days later we're out on the water, miles away from anyone, and a boat comes rushing out to meet us. Frank had an emergency call at the lodge where we were staying, so we packed up and rushed in." John sat back in his recliner with a heavy laugh and slapped his knee. "He was so angry when he put that phone back on its base. I thought he busted the only working phone at the lodge."

"It was Sylvie?" Marco asked.

"You bet it was," John said, still laughing. "Just checking in to see why his phone was off. She had an emergency party come out after him. Of all the crazy things."

"If Frank is on a fishing trip, where do you think he'd be?"

"Bass Lake. It's about an hour east of here. We usually rent a fishing cabin for the week."

"Can you give us the lodging information?" Marco asked.

"Sure can. I'll write it down before you leave."

"I'll take care of it," his wife said, rising. "I've got all the info you need."

"Have you been there to fish?" I asked her.

"Not to fish." She smiled at me. "John took me there once and that was enough for me. I don't fancy roughing it."

"Sally," John chided, "staying at a fishing lodge is hardly roughing it."

"It is to me," she replied.

John cleared his throat after his wife left the room. "There's probably something else I should mention. I don't like telling tales out of school, but Frank and Eileen have been having problems."

"Marital problems?" Marco asked.

John scratched his ear, looking uncomfortable. "Frank didn't say much about it, but he let me know things weren't running smoothly on the home front. From what he said, they'd go long stretches without talking to each other."

"Here you go," his wife said, handing me a piece of paper. "And don't pay any attention to him. John very much likes to tell tales, and every couple has their differences. Between you, me, and this carp on the wall, I think the fishing trips saved our marriage." She sat down on the armrest next to her husband and put her arm around him. "I'm sure Frank will be back soon."

I watched as the two shared a loving glance. It was true every couple had their differences, but I was glad that Marco and I were almost always on the same page. Even when we did disagree, we'd always been able to work it out. There was absolutely no sign of anything ever changing that.

Glancing at me, Marco said, "I think we have all we need."

I put the lodging information in my purse along with the notebook and pen and stood up. "Thanks for seeing us on such short notice."

"It's no problem at all," John said, walking us to the door. "I have to warn you, though. It won't be easy to locate him unless you want to call out a search party. I'd be happy to take you to the lodge myself if you'd like. I could show you some of the spots we frequent."

"I appreciate the offer," Marco said, shaking his hand. "I might take you up on that."

Back in the car, I buckled my seatbelt and asked Marco what he thought.

"I find it odd that Frank wouldn't have asked his best friend to go with him," he said.

"What bothered me is that he left without telling his sister or his best friend."

Marco started the engine. "But he did tell his wife."
"Or so she says."
"I'll reach out to Eileen Vesco tomorrow."

TARA

After dinner with my parents, I headed up to my room to study. It was a warm evening, so I opened the window before sitting down at my desk. I turned on the green-shaded desk lamp and dug my history book out of my bookbag. I opened it to chapter ten, took out my notebook and pencil, and bent my head over the book. A flash to the right caught my eye and I looked over to see the neighbors two yards down starting up a fire in their fire pit. Another couple joined them, and I watched enviously as they gathered around the fire, glasses in their hands, chatting and laughing.

I turned left to look at David's house. Through his window, I could see a tall figure standing in his room. For a moment I thought he was looking my way, so I put my head down quickly and swiped through a few pages of my history book. When I looked back up, the light in his room was turned off.

Then I saw a light come on directly opposite me and picked up my binoculars as Deena took a seat at her desk. I saw movement in the window below her, on the first floor, and looked down to see her father get out of his recliner and leave what appeared to be the family room. Moments later, Deena suddenly jumped up, went to her door, and shut it. I saw her lock her door, then sit back down at her desk. I put the binoculars down quickly so she wouldn't look over and see me using them.

And there I waited, wondering whether her father would knock, wondering whether Deena would open the door, but nothing happened. I picked up the binoculars again, focused on the family room, and finally saw the father return to his chair. I could see half of a matching recliner beside his, but it was empty. And once again I wondered where Deena's mother was.

From outside, just below my window, I heard a voice say, "I've heard of a peeping Tom, but never a peeping Tara."

I leaned over my desk to see down to the yard beneath me. And there stood David, his neck craned to look up at me. My heart stopped as I dropped the binoculars out of sight. "I have no idea what you're talking about." I was fully prepared to lie through my teeth about spying on him, but David wasn't angry. He was laughing.

"What are you doing up there?"

I couldn't help but smile back. "Don't move. I'll be right down."

I fairly danced down the stairs. As I rounded the corner into the hallway my mom called, "Where are you going?"

"Out back. A friend is out there."

"A friend?"

"Yes, Mom. David Harrison."

"Are you going to invite David inside?"

I paused. "No, Mom. You'll embarrass me."

I opened the back door, stepped out onto our deck, and triggered the motion-detecting floodlights. David was sitting on the low railing, a soft drink can in one hand, his other shielding his eyes from the bright light.

I took a seat beside him. "What are you doing outside in the dark?"

"Spying on you."

I could feel myself blushing. "Why are you spying on me?"

"I'm kidding!" he said emphatically. "The real question is, why were you spying on me?"

He had me there. Feeling like a complete idiot, not to mention a peeping Tom, I said with a shrug, "I wasn't spying on you. I just like to watch the birds."

Lame, Tara. I could tell by the look on his face that he wasn't buying it, so I came clean. "I'm writing an article for journalism class."

"Must be a slow news cycle." He took a swig from the can. "Are you writing about me?"

"No. I told you, I wasn't watching you. I mean, that's not why I have the binoculars."

"I saw you, Tara. I could see your desk light glaring off the lens."

"I mean, it wasn't you whom I was trying to watch."

"Then who?"

"The girl in the house next to yours. Deena Allen."

"Why?"

Did I dare tell him? Would he believe me?"

He sensed my hesitation. "What? What did you see?"

"Okay, don't think I'm crazy, but the other night, in the middle of the night, I saw Mr. Allen drag something through the backyard and into that tool shed over there."

David pondered it a few moments. "What did he drag?"

"Something long and bulky, something that looked like it was wrapped up in a blanket or heavy material. And here's the thing. I haven't seen any sign of Deena's mother lately."

David looked at me skeptically. "So what if you haven't seen her mother lately?"

"I just think it's odd that I wouldn't see her. I see Deena, her younger sister, and her dad, but not her mother."

"Do you spy on them all the time?"

"No."

"Then Isn't it possible that you're overreacting?"

Stupid, Tara. Why did you tell him?

I toyed with a button on my sweater. "I suppose."

He was quiet for a few seconds, then he suddenly set his can on the deck and rose. "Come on."

"What?"

"Come with me."

"Where?"

"Let's go check out that tool shed."

I followed him off the deck. Was this really happening? I caught up to him and we traipsed across my backyard into Deena's, stopping directly behind the shed. Next to us was an old pile of wood stacked up to my waist, dirty and covered in leaves. I stayed near the woodpile while David peered around the shed, then ducked back. "Okay, I can see Mr. *Wife Killer* sitting in his chair. We should be safe."

He snuck around the shed with me right behind him. There was a small window on the back side, but the glass had been broken and boarded over with wooden slats. We circled the shed, stopping in front of the shed's door where David lifted the heavy padlock. "No one's getting through this door, that's for sure."

"See what I mean? Why would he have a padlock on the shed?"

"Oh, come on, Tara. Who leaves a tool shed unlocked? He probably has a lawnmower and a lot of equipment inside."

"But why such a heavy-duty lock?"

"Seems like a normal padlock to me."

I folded my arms and huffed. Looking back at the window, I could still see Mr. Allen in the living room sitting in front of the soft, flickering glow of the television. The shed was far enough from the house that I wasn't worried about being seen in the dark but close enough that we could've been heard if we'd made a loud noise.

I checked the window on the backside, noticing that it had been hastily boarded up, leaving enough of a gap to see that the glass was broken. I turned on my flashlight app and shined the light inside. "Look."

David peered through the slats. "What am I looking at?"

"Does that look like a body?"

He took my phone, shined the light at different angles, and whispered. "Looks like a bag of leaves."

I took the phone back and looked again. Just a sliver of black plastic was visible. I let out a frustrated sigh. "We're never going to find out what's in this shed."

"Not unless we pick the lock."

I turned the flashlight off and pocketed my cell phone. "Do you know how to do that?"

He glanced at me in surprise. "I was joking."

"Oh. So was I."

"Right."

Before stepping away from the shed, we checked to make sure no one was watching, then walked across the yard to my house where David picked up his soda can. "I've got to get back. History test to study for." He started to walk away then turned back. "Don't you dare use those binoculars to watch me."

Now was the time for a snappy comeback, something to show him how clever I was, how witty, how perfect I was for him. Unfortunately, my brain had other ideas. Make that no ideas. Here I was in the presence of a guy I'd literally dreamed about and the best I could do was say, "No worries."

He winked at me. "See you around, Sherlock."

I watched him cross the backyard and head toward his house, and then it hit me. He'd been standing right there talking about the history exam. I could've asked him to study together. He could've invited me inside, maybe even up to his room where we could've been alone, but no, I blew it once again.

At least we'd had a chance to talk. That was a good first step. Smiling to myself, I walked back inside, ignored my mom, and floated up to my room. David had called me Sherlock. He'd nicknamed me, just like Marco had nicknamed Aunt Abby his sunshine. Had I found my very own Marco?

Keep dreaming, Tara.

Then another thought struck me. I parted the curtains and looked across the yard at Deena's bedroom window. Maybe David and I weren't the only ones struggling with our history exam.

CHAPTER FOUR

ABBY

Tuesday

Tuesday morning started as most mornings did, with a cup of Grace's freshly brewed java and a meeting in the parlor. Lottie, Rosa, and I had all brought in clothing for Grace's donation bin and felt very good about it. We also felt good about the number of orders that had come in overnight. Ten orders were just for a funeral that was to take place that afternoon at four o'clock at the Happy Dreams Funeral Parlor. Those orders were up first.

At ten o'clock, as Rosa and I were in the workroom making those arrangements, the purple curtain parted, and Jillian came through. As always, she was dressed in high fashion, a slender, long white coat with big black buttons down the front and black epaulets on the shoulders. To go with it, she wore black patent boots and a black patent shoulder bag. She was carrying a duffel bag, also in black.

"Good morning everyone," she called, tossing her purse onto my desk chair. "Guess what I brought?" She unzipped a sports bag and opened it up for us to see. Inside was a stack of neatly folded clothes. "It's for your donation bin. Just look at what I brought."

She pulled out one of the garments, a beautiful baby blue sweater, a perfect complement to her copper-colored hair.

"It's beautiful," Rosa gushed. "Some lucky woman will love it."

"Yes, I know," Jillian said and set it on the worktable. She pulled out another garment, a dress in forest green.

"That is also beautiful." Rosa sighed. "I wish I had such nice clothing."

Jillian pulled out several garments, all in high style, all in perfect condition. By that time, Grace and Lottie had stepped in to see the collection.

"What a generous donation," Lottie said.

"It reminds me of a quote," Grace said. She got into her lecture pose, her hands holding the edges of her cardigan, her chin high, her posture erect. "As that brilliant writer Henry Wadsworth Longfellow once said, 'Give what you have. To someone, it may be better than you dare to think.'"

"Good one, Gracie," Lottie said, patting her on the back. Grace was a veritable treasure trove of quotations.

Jillian was now holding the baby blue sweater in her hands, gazing at it longingly. "Okay," she said on a sigh. "I'll just take these into the shop and put them in the donation bin."

"Would you like help?" Grace asked.

"No, I can manage."

As Grace and Lottie left the room, Jillian put the blue sweater aside and scooped up everything else. "What?" she asked, at my puzzled look.

"Why did you put that one aside?"

"I think I'm going to keep it." She pushed through the curtain, her arms loaded with clothing.

I pulled another order, read it over, then stepped into the big cooler to pull my stems. When I stepped out, Jillian was back with the green dress.

"You're going to keep that one, too?" I asked.

"It complements my eyes."

I had a feeling we were going to have to hide the rest of her donations.

My cell phone rang, and Marco's name appeared on the screen. "Hi, honey. What's up?" I asked.

"We have an interview with Frank Vesco's wife this evening at seven-thirty. I had a hard time getting her to agree to it. She didn't sound thrilled to hear we were investigating her husband's whereabouts."

"Did she tell you anything?"

"I didn't get into any questions with her. We'll handle those this evening."

"Sounds good. And listen, if you don't want leftovers from last night, you'd better bring something home. It looks like I'll be staying until six again today."

"How does chili sound?"

"Delicious. It's the perfect day for it."

"Got it. See you tonight."

I hung up and pulled another order from the spindle. This was for a funeral wreath, so I went to the big cooler and looked at my stock. I finally settled on a monochromatic scheme of deep burgundy Dahlias, an orange-red Amaranthus, burgundy Celosias, and variegated ferns for my green accent. I took a wire form wreath from the top of a cabinet and set to work.

Rosa stuck her head through the curtain. "Your cousin is back."

I walked out to see Jillian digging through the donation bin. "What are you doing?"

She pulled out a black sweater with red accents. "I didn't mean to donate this."

Just then a young woman dressed in long khaki pants and a green jacket walked in. She spied the donation box then looked around.

"Can I help you?" I asked.

Grace came walking in from the tea parlor and wrapped the woman in a hug. "Jennifer, this is Abby Knight Salvare and her cousin, Jillian. Abby, this is Jennifer Moore from the women's shelter."

Jillian stepped back, clutching her black sweater.

"Abby," Jennifer said after introductions, "I can't thank you enough." She looked at the box overflowing with donations, topped with the items Jillian had yet to recover. "Wow, these are beautiful. You have no idea how helpful this will be. Some of the women who come to our shelter have nothing. It's generous donations like these that keep these women and their children clothed and cared for."

Grace helped Jennifer bag up the clothes, but before they could leave, Jillian stepped up and placed her sweater back in the donation bin. She gave me a faltering smile and left without saying a word.

✿❀✿

Sometime after three o'clock, my niece Tara came through the purple curtain almost wiggling with excitement. "Aunt Abby, I have to show you my story."

"Let me wrap up this arrangement first and then I'll take a look." I turned the anniversary bouquet in a circle to see if from all angles and smiled in satisfaction.

Tara hopped up onto a wooden stool at the worktable and pulled a folder out of her backpack. "I was chosen to write the feature article for the high school newspaper."

"Good for you!"

As I tore off a big sheet of wrapping paper, she pulled a piece of paper from the folder and slid it toward me. Lottie and I still had a lot of orders to do before the shop closed, but Tara was especially eager to show me her story. How could I refuse? It wasn't often that my niece stopped by after school to share something with me.

I finished wrapping the arrangement, set it in the big cooler, ready for delivery, then stood beside Tara. "Okay, let's see your paper."

"Now remember, this is my first attempt at a feature article."

"I'll keep that in mind." I read the paper and was amazed by her writing ability. After finishing, I put my arm around her shoulders and gave her an affectionate squeeze. "Good job, Tara. I can see why your teacher chose you. This is really creative."

"Well, see, that's the thing. I didn't *create* this story. It's based on real life."

That made me pause. "I don't understand. Whose life?"

Tara put the paper back into the folder. "There's a girl who lives in the house across the backyard from me. Deena Allen. Her father is the man I wrote about."

"He's the man you saw drag something bulky through his backyard?"

Tara nodded. "In the middle of the night. And into this big tool shed in his backyard. And here's another thing. Ever since then I've been watching Deena's room and just like in my article," -Tara leaned toward me to say in a hushed voice, "her mother never appears." She leaned back, lifting her eyebrows.

I picked up a pair of shears and began snipping the bottoms of several mums. "That doesn't mean her mother was murdered. Maybe she simply talks to Deena in the kitchen while she's making dinner. Or after dinner. She doesn't have to go to Deena's room, does she?"

"Aunt Abby, listen to me." Tara put her palms on the tabletop. "Several times Deena has slammed the door in her father's face. Hard. And the mother *never comes to see why*."

"Maybe she knows why."

Tara made a disgusted sound. "You don't get it. When I saw what was happening at Deena's, something inside of me was practically buzzing, like an alarm is going off. I can't explain it, but I know something is wrong."

"You feel it like an internal antenna?"

"Yes!" Tara said. "Just like that. Like something is wrong and I have to fix it."

I watched as my niece gripped the table and stared at me, the intense expression on her face so eerily familiar that I put the sheers down and sat next to her. "I get that feeling, too."

"You do?"

"Yes, but I have to tell you that I'm not always right. Intuition can be a very powerful tool if you know how to use it, but you have to be careful. Your imagination can get in the way."

"I'm not imagining this. Something is wrong and I need your help."

"Tara, I'd love to help you, but I think you need a little more information, just to make sure there isn't a simpler answer."

She slid off the stool, put her paper in her backpack, and shot me a glare. "Of all people, I thought *you* would get it." And with that, she stormed through the purple curtain. Moments later I heard the bell above the shop's door ring.

Lottie came through the curtain carrying a handful of order slips. "What was that about?"

"Tara thinks her neighbor killed his wife."

"Oh, Lordy," Lottie said with a sigh. "Looks like we have a budding amateur detective on our hands."

I thought about that as Lottie stuck the orders on the spindle on my desk. Tara was fond of saying she wanted to be just like me, catching murderers and solving mysteries. Was this her attempt at that? Was she seeing a crime where there was none?

Lottie took off her yellow bib apron and slipped on her jacket. "I've got to make more deliveries, sweetie. Rosa is handling the customers up front and Grace is in the coffee and tea parlor serving a book club group."

"Thanks, Lottie."

After dinner and a walk with Seedy that evening, Marco and I headed out to Frank Vesco's house for a seven-thirty appointment with his wife. We pulled up in front of a narrow, two-story, brown brick house and parked. "All set?" Marco asked.

"I'm ready when you are."

Eileen Vesco opened the door before we could ring the doorbell.

"Marco Salvare," my husband said. "We spoke on the phone. This is my wife and partner Abby."

She didn't smile. "Come in."

Eileen Vesco was a stunning looking woman in her mid-forties, with long, luxurious dark hair, large dark eyes, and ruby lips. She appeared to be dressed to go out, wearing a deep red sweater with a black skirt and black pumps, the outfit complementing her dark good looks.

Rather than take us into the living room off to the right side of the entrance hall, where I saw a pumpkin-colored candle burning on the coffee table, she led us into a dining room furnished with a cherry wood dining table, eight chairs, and tall hutch. The air was redolent with the smell of barbequed beef, making me hungry all over again.

"Have a seat," she said.

Marco and I sat side by side at the table and Eileen sat opposite us, her arms crossed, looking very put out. "I suppose you're here because of my sister-in-law."

"Yes, we are," Marco said. "Mrs. Freeman is worried about her brother."

She huffed in exasperation. "Worried about her brother to the point of hiring a private detective? Even though I told her that Frank is on a fishing trip?"

"She finds it odd that her brother hasn't returned her phone calls," Marco said.

Eileen sighed loudly and rolled her eyes. "Sylvie Freeman is a busybody. She sits around her empty house and fusses over nothing. She has to keep track of everyone and everything. The entire Vesco family finds her irritating, most especially Frank."

"Can you elaborate?" I asked, my pen and notebook ready.

"Sylvie used to phone Frank every evening just to gossip. Frank finally limited her to every other evening and even that irked him. And then there are her text messages. Sometimes a dozen will come in on Saturdays when Sylvie knows Frank is home. She can't stand it if he doesn't reply right away."

I wrote it down.

"Is it common for Frank to take a week off to fish?" Marco asked.

"Oh, yes. He loves fishing. He has a very busy accounting business so he squeezes in a fishing trip whenever he can. But I suspect what he enjoys more is a reason to put his phone away and hide from his sister."

"Have you heard from Frank this week?" Marco asked.

"I heard from him last Monday evening, once he'd settled into the cabin."

"And since then?"

"I had a text message from him on Sunday saying he'd decided to stay for a few more days. He said the weather was perfect and the fishing was great."

"Can he take off work that long?" I asked.

"His nephew Michael can cover for him. Michael works for Frank."

"Michael Vesco?" I asked.

"No, Porter."

I wrote down Michael's name.

"At what point would you start to worry about Frank?" Marco asked.

"Let's see. Today is Tuesday. I suppose if I didn't hear from him by Friday I'd start to worry."

"Okay," Marco said, "I think that will do it."

"I'm sorry Sylvie sent you on a wild goose chase," Eileen added. "Let her know that I've heard from Frank and all is well. I'd tell her myself, but obviously she doesn't trust me."

We thanked her and left. Once we were in the car and buckled in, I said, "What did you think?"

"After hearing what Eileen had to say, I get the distinct feeling that Frank's sister is a worrywart."

"What are you going to tell Sylvie?"

"Nothing yet. I want to talk to Michael Porter and get his take on his uncle's absence." Marco pulled the car away from the curb.

I glanced back at Frank Vesco's house. "You know what? I don't trust Eileen. She was too calm about her husband's long absence. If you were gone that long on a fishing trip, I'd begin to suspect something *fishy* was going on."

"Like what?"

"Like a secret girlfriend."

"Abby, I'd be crazy to have a secret girlfriend when I have a wife like you."

"You mean a hard-headed, hot-blooded, amateur detective wife like me?"

Marco laughed. "I mean a beautiful, smart, amazing wife like you."

"Good save, Salvare."

"I can see Eileen's side of the story, but I have to wonder why Frank hasn't communicated with his sister or his fishing buddy." Marco pulled the phone from his pocket and asked me to find the number for Michael Porter. "I'd like to get his take on Frank's absence. Even if Frank's sister is a worrywart, something seems wrong with that picture."

I searched for the Vesco accounting firm and found the number for Michael Porter. The call went to voicemail, so I left a message.

We continued to discuss the case on the way home, and I wrote up a list of questions for Frank's nephew. Even though my intuition was telling me that Frank's wife was more involved than she'd let on, I had to remind myself of the advice I'd given Tara. Intuition is powerful, but so is imagination.

Seedy and Smoke were starved for attention when we got home, so Marco found a few toys and began to play while I poured two glasses of wine.

"Tara came to see me today," I said. "She wanted to show me the journalism article that she wrote."

Marco didn't comment as he bent down to scratch Seedy behind the ears, so I continued. "She was supposed to make up the article but instead she wrote about something she saw from her bedroom window."

Smoke joined the fun by pouncing on Seedy with a playful meow. Our clever little dog rolled over to play dead, and when Smoke turned away, she quickly got her three legs under her and chased Smoke down the hallway.

"So," I said, trying to get his attention, "Tara wrote about a murder."

Marco straightened. "What about a murder?"

"What she thinks was an actual murder."

Marco joined me and picked up his wine from the kitchen island. "Tara thinks she saw a murder?"

"Not the actual murder but the aftermath."

"Is she serious?"

"Very serious. She saw the man who lives across the backyard dragging something bulky across his yard and into a tool shed in the middle of the night. She also said she hasn't seen the wife lately."

Marco's phone rang in his pocket and he answered quickly after seeing the number on the screen.

I stood at the kitchen counter watching my handsome hubby, but my mind was still pondering Tara's story. Why would anyone have to drag something to a shed in the middle of the night? I'm sure there were many reasons, but nothing logical came to mind.

"That was Michael Porter. He can meet with us tomorrow at noon if you can get away."

"I think I can manage that."

"Maybe we should go over the list of questions tonight."

"Okay, but I'm still wondering about Tara's story. I think she raises some good questions."

Marco shook his head. "I think she's being nosy."

"She made a convincing case in her newspaper article."

"She's been hanging out with her Aunt Abby too much. You don't buy into her theory, do you?"

"Of course not," I told him, feeling a little cut short. "It's just a homework assignment. But she's got the Knight family talent for snooping, that's for sure."

"I hope she's not going to snoop any further."

"I doubt she has any plans for that."

CHAPTER FIVE

TARA

Wednesday

I had a plan.

At lunch, I went to the cafeteria, got my food, and looked around. My friends waved at me and I wiggled my elbow at them but didn't join them. I was looking for Deena Allen.

I pivoted in a circle, searching the tables full of students, and finally saw Deena sitting by herself, reading a textbook. I walked over to the table and stood opposite her holding my tray. "Mind if I join you?"

She looked up at me, shrugged, and went back to reading.

I set my tray down and slid onto a chair. "I'm Tara Knight. You live in the house behind mine. We share a backyard."

Her gaze moved up over me, studying me curiously. "Hi."

Deena had long, dark hair wound in tiny curls down the sides of her face. She wore the same red sweater I had seen her wearing before, but there was a stain on the collar, and it looked like her shirt underneath was wrinkled. She was plain-looking, or at least, her solemn expression shrouded her more attractive features. She had big, dark eyes and thin lips, was a little taller than me, and didn't seem like she wanted my company.

"Aren't you in my homeroom?" I asked.

"Yes." She said it as a question.

"I just wanted to introduce myself. I'm sorry I didn't do it sooner."

"That's okay." She picked up a brownie from her lunch tray and took a large bite. Between chewing, she said, "I think you're in my geometry class, too."

I looked over the items on her tray. Pizza, fries, milk, and two brownies. I also noticed she was reading her geometry book, with notes scattered next to her with highlighted instructions. "I hate geometry. How about you?"

She shrugged again and kept her eyes glued to the pages of her book. "I don't understand it."

I unpacked my lunch from a small paper bag. I took a bite of my ham sandwich and chewed it thoughtfully. I'd planned to get close to Deena, use my wit and charm to win her over, and extract some information from her, but it seemed as though my wit and charm were lost on Deena. "I feel your pain. I'm the same way with history class, all the dates and names, it's just too much to remember."

Deena didn't respond. She finished the last bite of her brownie and started on the second, not even having touched the pizza or fries. I found that extremely odd. She finally swallowed and said, "Same. I hate history."

"Hey, maybe we could study for our history exam together."

She looked up from her book. "Who do you have, Mrs. Strayer or Mr. Flaherty?"

"Mrs. Strayer."

"I have Flaherty." She shook her head. "Different teachers. Different tests."

There went that plan. I had hoped to get a little insight into the Allen household while also possibly studying for a test that I'd desperately needed help with, but Deena was right. Different teachers had different tests.

Deena closed her geometry book with a frustrated sigh. "I just don't get it."

"Maybe I could help you. I love geometry."

She looked at me quizzically. "You literally just said you hated it."

What had I just said? I didn't love geometry. I was a writer, not a mathematician, but I was desperate, and I had to come up with an answer before Deena got up and left. "I do hate it – it's a love/hate relationship, really – but I understand it, so . . ."

"Really?"

"Yeah, you know, I could help you if you want."

She seemed to perk up at that. "That'd be cool."

"Why don't you come over after supper this evening and I'll help you with the homework?"

She looked startled for an instant then picked up her milk carton and toyed with it. "I can't come over tonight." She dropped her gaze. "Maybe tomorrow."

"But the homework is due tomorrow."

Deena picked up her tray and scooted her chair back. "I can't tonight. I'm sorry."

As I watched her walk away, I got the feeling that something was terribly wrong. The antenna that Aunt Abby had mentioned was buzzing loudly. I had to come up with a new plan.

ABBY

Marco picked me up at noon for the ten-minute ride to an office building just south of town in an industrial park. Famished, I ate my turkey sandwich quickly and even had time to apply a nude lipstick before we headed into the modern glass and brick building. Inside, we found a directory on the wall and located Vesco Accounting, Ltd on the third floor.

We took an ultra-quiet elevator and stepped off into a carpeted hallway decorated with large, colorful art prints on the walls. There were several glass-fronted doors in the hallway, so we proceeded along until we found a door with *Vesco Accounting, Ltd.* printed on it. Inside, a receptionist seated at a very modern wood and black metal desk glanced up from her computer monitor and smiled. "May I help you?"

"We're here to see Michael Porter," Marco said.

"He'll be finished in just a few minutes. Please have a seat in the waiting area."

We had just sat down on a bank of seats across from the receptionist when a door opened up a hallway and a tall, thin man came out with an elderly couple. He showed the couple to the door, said goodbye, and disappeared back into his room. Several minutes later, a different door opened, and a young man came out with a middle-aged couple.

"I'll be in touch as soon as I have everything ready," he told them.

They thanked him and left. He went over to the receptionist's desk, bent over to study something, then straightened and looked our way.

"Mr. and Mrs. Salvare?"

It still gave me a thrill to hear myself called by my married name. Inside, I would always be Abby Knight, but to the world, I was Mrs. Abby Salvare.

"Come in, please," the man said, allowing us to enter before him. "Have a seat."

We walked past a closed door that had *Frank Vesco* printed on it. Inside Michael's office, we sat on two leather chairs in front of a big maple desk. Michael introduced himself as he sat and pulled himself up to the desk. He was a handsome man, with light brown hair, deep blue eyes, and a crisp gray suit with a white shirt and gray-and-red striped tie.

"You said on the phone you had questions about my uncle's absence," Michael said. "How can I help?"

While I took out the notebook and pen, Marco started the questioning. "Sylvie Freeman, I believe she's your aunt, contacted us because she's worried. She said it was unusual for Frank not to call her back or return her text messages, especially after an entire week of being away. What is your take on that?"

Michael cleared his throat. "Aunt Sylvie does tend to exaggerate, and she does phone Uncle Frank a lot. With that said, however, I do think it's a bit odd that he wouldn't let me know he was extending his trip."

"How did you learn about his extended trip?"

"Aunt Eileen let me know."

"Are you worried at all about those extra days being out of the ordinary?"

"He's done it before, and I can handle the business . . ."

"But?"

"But I wish he'd call me, just to, you know, check in."

"How often does your uncle take off for a fishing trip?"

"I'd estimate about seven or eight times a year."

"That's a lot of trips," Marco said.

"He loves fishing. It's a passion with Uncle Frank."

"Does he usually go by himself?"

"Not usually, no."

Marco's rapid-fire questions had me practically scribbling the answers.

"Are you aware that he went without his fishing buddy this time?"

"He went without John?"

"Does that surprise you?" Marco asked.

Michael lifted his shoulders and let them drop casually. "It's unusual, but if he wanted to go alone, then I'm sure he had his reasons."

I noted that he didn't seem too concerned.

"If something were to happen to your uncle," Marco said, "what would happen to the business?"

Very coolly he answered, "I don't think anything happened to him. I think Sylvie is overly concerned, but if something were to happen, I would run the business. He's been training me to take over for him one day."

"Would his wife or children inherit it?" Marco asked.

"Uncle Frank doesn't have any children."

"Then it would go to his wife?"

Michael paused. "Actually," -he toyed with a pen on the desktop- "Uncle Frank is leaving it to me."

I was stunned. Frank was leaving a lucrative business to his nephew and not his wife? I wrote it down.

"If Frank doesn't return this week," Marco asked, "at what point would you become alarmed?"

"I'd say by the end of the week. That would be nearly two full weeks of him being away." Michael adjusted his tie. "But I'm certain he'll be back before then."

Marco glanced at me and I closed the notebook. "I think that's all we have," he said. "Is there anything you can think of that we should know about your uncle?"

"Nope. Just that he's a fine businessman and a devoted husband."

"Okay." Marco shook his hand. "Thanks for seeing us."

Before we left, Michael added, "There is something you should know about Aunt Sylvie, though. She tends to do this, to overreact to situations that are out of her control. She's also on a fixed income, so keep that in mind before you start taking more money from her."

As we rode down in the elevator I said, "Why was I sensing something artificial in Michael's behavior?"

"I sensed it, too, Abby. He was playing down Frank's absence, as though he didn't want us to be concerned."

"Maybe Sylvie is wrong and there's nothing to be concerned about. Eileen Vesco certainly wasn't. But Michael did seem a little embarrassed to tell us he would inherit the business."

"I wonder how Frank's wife feels about that," Marco said.

"I was wondering the same thing."

We stepped out of the elevator and headed toward the exit. "Michael inheriting his uncle's business could be a motive," I said. "Maybe Michael wanted the business sooner rather than later."

"Don't get ahead of yourself, Abby. Frank is just missing at this point." Marco opened the glass door for me, and we walked outside. "But if Sylvie Freeman doesn't hear from her brother by tomorrow, we may need to take a trip up to the fishing cabin."

"The problem is, I don't know when I'd be able to get away."

Marco unlocked the car door with his key fob. "Then maybe I'll call John and have him take me up there."

TARA

I had a new plan.

The hallways were noisy and jammed after school, but I found Deena standing alone at her locker. "Hey, there," I said, sidling up next to her. "How are you?"

She looked confused. "Fine."

"Because you seemed a little upset at lunch."

"I'm sorry," she said. "Just a lot going on right now."

"The offer still stands, if you need help with geometry."

"I can't come over tonight. I can't leave my sister at home alone."

"Why don't I come over to your house?"

Even though Deena seemed to be warming up to me, she still had a hard time looking me in the eye. She closed her locker, zipped up her bookbag, and hefted it around her shoulders. "You want to come to my house?"

"Yeah, why not?"

She was hesitant but finally cracked a small smile. "I guess that would be okay."

"Great! I can be there around seven."

"Okay," Deena said. "Come to the back door."

"Oh, and I was talking to my mom this morning and she wants to have your mother over for coffee."

Deena turned and stared at me. "Why?"

"Well, I guess to welcome you to the neighborhood."

Deena quickly averted her gaze. "I – it's – it's really kind of your mom to invite us, but-" She paused as though trying to find a way to end her sentence.

"It would be a good way for your mom to make a new friend," I said.

"It's just that my mom is – she's away. I don't think it's going to work out." Deena swiveled and began walking briskly down the hallway.

I took a few strides to catch up with her, thinking of my next move. "How long will your mom be gone?"

"Oh, a while. She's visiting family. I really can't say for how long."

"Where did she go?"

"Colorado."

"That's cool. Where in Colorado? I've been to Denver."

"Not Denver. Just some town you've probably never heard of." She stopped in her tracks, her face burning bright red. "I have to go. Band practice."

"No problem."

I watched her hurry away. And that's just what she'd done, hurry away as soon as I started asking questions about her mother. If something *had* happened to her mother, would she be covering it up? Or maybe she'd made up the Colorado story because she was *afraid* of what had happened to her mother.

Another possibility was that her father had told her the *helping out the family* story and that was what she was repeating. But it was obvious by her evasiveness that she wasn't buying it. So the question remained, where was Mrs. Allen?

I had to get Aunt Abby on board.

CHAPTER SIX

ABBY

At three-thirty that afternoon, I was working on a get-well arrangement of yellow forsythia, yellow pansies, and yellow daffodils, when my mom popped into the workroom with a big smile on her face. She was wearing her standard teacher's outfit of a pair of neutral-colored pants, a matching print blouse, and tan flats. "I see some of my candles sold."

"Three so far," I told her. "People seem to like the food theme."

"I'm so glad. I was a little nervous about how they'd go over. I've got more at home. I'll bring them by on Friday."

The curtain parted and Tara practically skipped into the room. She had on a pair of blue jeans and a denim jean jacket with a green T-shirt underneath, her bright red hair pulled back with a scrunchie. "Hi, grandma. Hi Aunt Abby."

My mom gave her a hug. "What brings you here?"

Tara set her bookbag on my desk chair and scooted onto a wooden stool across from where I was working. "I just, you know, wanted to stop by to see how things were going."

That was shorthand for *I need to talk to Aunt Abby.*

Tara scrunched her nose and looked around. "It smells like Mexican food in here."

"Isn't it lovely?" my mom asked. "Those are my dinner candles. They're out front on the big oak table."

"Oh, awesome. They smell great." Tara folded her hands on the slate worktable and looked at me, trying to hide her smile. After a brief pause, the silence became awkward.

My mom looked from Tara to me and got the picture. "Okay, I'll leave you two girls to talk. Abigail, I'll see you on Friday."

"Thanks, Mom."

Tara was fairly wiggling with excitement as my mom left the room. As soon as the curtain had dropped, she leaned forward. "Remember the neighbor I wrote about? Mr. Allen? Remember the daughter named Deena who keeps shutting the door in her father's face? Well, guess what? I've made friends with Deena and I got invited over to her house. And guess what else? Still no mother.

"She doesn't have a mother?"

"Deena *has* a mother. I used to see her in the garden all the time. But now there's no mother there. I'm telling you, Aunt Abby, that woman is gone. I've been watching for her and she isn't there."

"Have you been to her house?"

"No."

"Then how can you be sure her mother isn't there?"

Tara hesitated.

I could tell by her expression that she was embarrassed about something. I knew her too well. "How do you know she's gone, Tara?"

"Their windows are open."

"Tara."

"What? It's not spying if the windows are open. From my bedroom, I can see her father sitting alone in their family room watching TV. And when Deena's little sister came to her room, she was crying. Deena closed the door and held her. Not her mom. Not her dad. Deena." Tara took a breath. "Now what does that tell you?"

"That is odd."

"Thank you! Now here's where it gets odder. I invited Deena's mom to come over to have coffee with my mom, but

Deena made up an excuse about her mother being away in Colorado helping family."

"How do you know it's an excuse? Maybe that's where she really is."

"No way. You had to be there to see Deena trying to make the story sound believable. And when I asked her how long her mom would be gone, she didn't know. She did not know, Aunt Abby. If your mom left to go visit family, wouldn't she say how long she would be gone?"

"You have a point, but –"

"And guess what else? I did a little sleuthing. Actually, David and I did a little sleuthing. We snuck over to check out the tool shed that Mr. Allen dragged something into."

"Who's David?"

She smiled. "He's just a friend who lives next door to Deena." Tara stopped talking and her eyes drifted away. "He caught me using my binoculars on Deena's house and came over to see what was going on."

"He what?" I put down my snippers.

"I mean . . . he wasn't mad."

"You're spying on the neighbors with binoculars?"

"I looked it up. It's not illegal."

"Tara, if David caught you, think about what would happen if Deena's father caught you. Even if nothing suspicious was going on, I can't imagine he'd like that. He might even complain to your folks."

"Don't worry. I'm careful."

"Apparently, not that careful."

"Anyway," Tara said, brushing aside my comment, "we went over to look at the tool shed – and don't worry, it was dark – but the shed has this giant padlock on it so no one can get inside."

I had to admit, Tara had my mind working in overdrive. What if she was right? What if Deena's father had dragged a body to the shed in the middle of the night? What if Deena's mother really was missing? "I'd sure love to get a look inside that shed."

Oops. Had I said that out loud?

"Me, too!" Tara cried. "I'm telling you; we need to investigate."

"Let's start simple," I said. "Why don't you try to find out Deena's mother's name? Then we'll look her up on Facebook or Instagram and see what we can learn about her."

Tara slid off the stool, her whole face aglow with happiness. "I am so on it! I'm going to Deena's house tonight after dinner." She came around the table and threw her arms around me. "Thank you, Auntie A. We're going to make an *awesome* team."

✿❀✿

"Abby, I think Tara's making a big deal out of nothing."

I picked up our dinner plates and took them to the sink to rinse. "That's what I thought at first, Marco, but the more I think about it, the more suspicious I get."

We had just finished dinner, where I'd laid out all of Tara's findings to get Marco's opinion. I could tell by the doubt in his eyes, however, that he wasn't on board.

"First of all," he said, "from what I remember, it's pretty common to find a teenager at odds with one or both of her parents. Shutting the door on her dad isn't that strange."

I had to concede the point. "Second of all?" I asked.

"As far as the locked shed goes, I would think that for anyone storing expensive equipment outside, such as a riding mower, that a lock would be normal. I'd lock a tool shed if we had one."

Marco almost had me convinced. "Then how would you explain Mr. Allen dragging something to the shed in the middle of the night?"

He thought about it as I stacked dishes in the dishwasher. "There's a thousand reasonable explanations. Maybe he doesn't sleep well. Maybe he decided to finish up some yard work since he was awake."

"What kind of yard work would entail dragging something long and bulky and wrapped in material into a tool shed at three in the morning?"

Marco was quiet. I finally had him thinking.

He poured more wine into his glass and took a thoughtful sip. "Okay, that does sound strange, but since everything else has a logical explanation, I'm sure that does, too."

"I disagree."

"Are you going to encourage Tara to pursue this?"

"No, but I don't want her snooping around by herself."

"And what about the case we're working on now? You barely have time for that."

I kissed him on the cheek. "Don't worry. I'll make it work."

TARA

At seven on the nose, I was at Deena's back door, my backpack on my back. She opened the door and gave a start, not expecting to see me right there. She stepped back to let me enter and I walked in, trying to take everything in without seeming to.

The kitchen was neat and tidy. No dishes sitting on the gray marbled counter, no food on the dark wood table. White cabinets were clean and sparkling. Through a doorway off the kitchen, I caught a glimpse of another room with a fireplace. I suspected that was the family room where I'd seen her father sitting in his chair. The chair was empty, and I didn't hear a TV on.

I followed Deena through the kitchen and up a hallway past a living room to the staircase. I glanced into the living room very quickly but didn't see anyone. We traipsed upstairs past a closed door and stopped at her bedroom. The room had a twin bed in it with a peach-colored bedspread. The walls were also painted peach. Against the window in the back of the room was the desk where I'd seen her studying. I did a quick scan. No mess to be seen anywhere. The room was as neat and tidy as the kitchen.

She sat on the side of the bed and I did the same, taking a yellow notebook out of my backpack.

"Where do we start?" she asked.

That was a good question. I wanted to start by asking where her father was, and maybe follow up with where her mother had disappeared to, but instead, I took the geometry book from my bag and waited for the right time.

About an hour and a half into faking my way through geometry homework, Deena's little sister came into the room, stopping just inside to gaze at me shyly.

"Hi," I said. "I'm Tara."

"I'm Joy."

"It's nice to meet you, Joy."

She smiled at me. She was a pretty little girl with dark hair and a round face. "Dee, will you come help me?"

"Sure, sweetie." Deena got up, saying, "I'll be right back."

I was surprised that Deena hadn't seemed to mind the interruption at all. Still, I couldn't understand why Joy hadn't asked her mother for help. Or her father, for that matter. It sure seemed to me like something was very wrong here. And then I remembered my new mission was to get Deena's mother's name for Aunt Abby.

I rose and went to stand at the window, leaning over to check out the view of my house. My light wasn't on so I couldn't see into my room, but I could see my mom in the kitchen, just a tiny figure from that distance. She was still recognizable, though. I had to be more careful when I was looking out of my window.

Deena came back a short time later shaking her head. "Just some math problems Joy couldn't get." She smiled. "At least I understand *fifth-grade* math."

After an hour of faking my way through geometry homework, I was just about to ask Deena about her mother but was interrupted when her cell phone rang. She checked it and said, "I'll be right back."

I smiled at her. "No problem."

She stepped out into the hallway and pulled the door partway shut, leaving just enough of a gap for me to eavesdrop.

"Hi, Grandma."

It quickly became obvious that Deena's grandmother was upset because Deena kept saying, 'Okay, Grandma, calm down." Then she said in a hushed voice, "She went on a church retreat. I don't know why she didn't tell you. No, she can't call you. Dad says they're not supposed to communicate with anyone. Yes, I know that sounds strange."

They weren't supposed to communicate with anyone? Not even with their children? It sounded strange to me, too. What worried me more was that Deena's grandmother had not been told about the retreat. Wouldn't it be natural to tell your mother when you planned to be incommunicado for a week?

Then Deena said, "Joy is fine. Don't worry, okay? I love you, Grandma. I'll talk to you soon."

When she came back into the room, I narrowed my eyes and pretended to be concentrating hard on the homework. I looked up and said as innocently as I could, "Everything all right?"

"Yep."

And that was it. But it sure left a lot of questions in my mind.

Just then, a large man appeared in the doorway. "Deena, I think you'd better call it a night."

She shot him a furious glare, got up, and closed the door, saying as she did so, "We were just about finished."

Feeling awkward, I tore out the pages in my notebook on which I'd written notes and handed them to her. "Here. You keep them."

"I really appreciate your help," Deena said with a smile. She had finally warmed up to me.

As we approached the back door, I heard a TV on and glanced into the family room to see Deena's father sitting in a recliner watching the television. As I suspected, the other recliner was unoccupied. He was alone.

He stood up and walked toward us. "Hey, thanks for helping Deena, . . ." He paused and reached for my hand.

I looked at his outstretched arm and could only imagine him dragging a dead body through the yard. "Tara," I said, pulling my hands up to grip the straps of my backpack. "Tara Knight."

He dropped his hand and gave me a stiff smile. His hair was thick and combed back off his forehead. He had deep creases down the sides of his mouth and dark, soulless eyes. "Thanks, Tara. I know Deena appreciates it."

Deena turned to her dad. There was an unspoken tension as she stared him down. Feeling extremely awkward, I averted my gaze and happened to notice a long wooden key holder next to the back door. My eyes quickly scanned the keys, stopping on one in particular. I moved closer and squinted. There it was. The shed key.

Deena opened the door and stepped out onto the back porch with me. "Thanks again, Tara."

"You're very welcome." I stepped off the porch, turned to give her a little wave, and saw her father watching me out the window.

I know what you're up to, I thought as I stared right back at him. *And I'll find out what happened to your wife.* It was then I realized that I still hadn't gotten Deena's mother's name.

But at least I knew where the shed key was.

CHAPTER SEVEN

ABBY

Thursday

"What's this?"

I stopped making the bed and turned to find Marco standing over a laundry basket filled with clothes. "Donations for the women's shelter."

"Why is my old sweatshirt in with women's clothing?"

"Because sometimes women come to the shelter with their children. Grace said they need clothing of all sizes, even for teenage boys. So I went through your drawers and pulled out a couple of old things."

Marco was still digging through the basket. He pulled out a Cubs T-shirt. "You're giving this away?"

"Marco you've been wearing that since before I met you. I think you can spring for a new one."

Grumbling under his breath he put it back. Then he pulled out a gray hoodie and held it up. "Not this, Abby. This is my favorite hoodie. It has memories attached to it."

"Memories of what?"

"Just . . . memories."

I huffed. "Fine. Keep it."

He straightened, holding the hooded sweatshirt out in front of him, gazing at it like a prized possession. Then he stuck it back in a dresser drawer and closed it. "Just so you know, I'll be away most of the day. John is taking me to Bass Lake."

"I'm sorry I can't go with you." I pulled him in for a quick kiss. "Let me know what you find out."

At ten o'clock that morning, Jillian came into Bloomers with her husband in tow. Both were carrying huge, overstuffed black plastic bags. "Good morning," she sang out cheerfully, as Grace, Lottie, Rosa, and I all stopped what we were doing to watch. The customers Lottie had just rung up paused at the door to watch, too.

Jillian set her bag down beside the donation bin and had Claymore do the same. "Thank you, darling," she said and gave him a peck. Claymore raised his hand to say hello and goodbye to us, and left the shop, the bell over the door chiming merrily.

"Are those all clothes?" Rosa asked, staring at the giant bags.

"Of course." Jillian opened one up and let her peer inside. "And mostly mine."

"You'll have plenty of room in the bin," Grace said. "I took a load of clothes to the shelter yesterday after work."

"You'll have to take another load this evening, Grace," Jillian said. "And wait till the women get a look at *these* clothes. All designer stuff. I emptied my closets."

It did indeed look like she'd completely cleaned out her closets. However, I remembered how hard a time she'd had letting go of some of her things before and was a little cautious. "Are you sure about this, Jillian?"

"More than sure. Last night when I got home and saw my closet overflowing with clothes, I couldn't stop thinking about those women at the shelter. They need these more than me, so I've decided to give it all away."

"I can't believe it," Lottie said under her breath.

"And I'm going to start the six-item challenge," Jillian said joyfully.

"What's the six-item challenge, love?" Grace asked.

The customers stepped closer to hear.

"You have six basic pieces," Jillian explained. "Two bottoms, such as one skirt and one pair of pants in a neutral color. One dress, also neutral but black is best. Then you have three tops, like two shirts and one blazer or cardigan. You're allowed three extra items, such as a scarf and two pieces of jewelry. And that's it. You have to mix and match the pieces all week long. And the next week, you switch them around and wear them differently."

By the look on her face, Jillian apparently thought this was a brilliant idea. I, on the other hand, had deep reservations. "What if you get tired of your six pieces?"

"You have to be creative, that's all," she said with a smile. "And just imagine the joy those women will have when they open these bags."

"This is extremely generous of you, Jillian," Grace said.

"Oh, and there are baby items in the bags, too, Grace," Jillian added.

"May I just tell you," began the woman customer, "what a giving person you are? I'm going to go right home and clean out my closet, too. I love the idea of a six-item challenge."

"I've never heard of it," I said.

"Google it," Jillian responded. "It's an actual thing."

While Grace sat at the computer to figure out a donation receipt, Jillian followed me into the workroom and watched as I pulled an order from the spindle.

"Here's my first outfit," she said, and took off her long coat so I could see her black skirt and white shirt striped in very faint black and blue alternating stripes. "I can wear the shirt with jeans, too."

"I don't know, Jill. I can't see you being happy with only six choices."

Jillian accepted the receipt from Grace, stuck it in her purse, and gave me a frown. "Then you don't know me very well, Abs." She turned on her heel and left.

"The thing is," I said to Grace, "I do know her very well. And I say she won't last a week."

TARA

I found Deena sitting by herself at the back of the cafeteria. My mission was clear: Get Deena's mother's name so I could help Aunt Abby search for her online. As I approached, I could see that Deena had a tray full of food but was once again eating the brownie first. Before I had a chance to sit down, I felt a hand grab my shoulder and spin me around. "David?"

"Come with me."

The butterflies in my stomach pulled me forward as I followed David out of the cafeteria, still holding my sack lunch. He turned the corner and stopped by the trophy case, the light illuminating his silky hair and bright eyes. I was forced out of my trance when he opened his bookbag and pulled out a box full of locks. "What's this?"

"It's a lock pick practice set. I ordered it online."

My eyes grew large as he unfolded the tiny interchangeable key parts. "You bought a lock pick set? Do you know how to use it?"

"Not at all, but I've been watching YouTube videos. How hard can it be?"

I picked up a few picks and toyed with the clear lock. "Seems pretty hard to me."

"Let's try it out tonight."

"Seriously?"

"You want to get a look inside that shed, don't you? This is the only way."

I couldn't hide my smile. I didn't dare tell him that I'd found the key to the shed. He went through all this trouble just for me. How could I say no?

"Give me your number and I'll text you tonight at midnight. Don't fall asleep."

As I read my phone number aloud, I could barely conceal my excitement. This was actually happening.

"I'll see you tonight, Sherlock."

ABBY

Mid-afternoon, Marco texted me to let me know he was on his way home from Bass Lake and would be at the house by six o'clock. Rosa and I worked like fiends to finish up the orders that needed to go out that day and Lottie made deliveries all afternoon.

Tara came in after school, dropped her bookbag, hopped up on a stool, and said, "I got it! I got Deena's mother's name! Now ask me how."

I was about to tie a bow on an anniversary arrangement and paused. "How?"

"I sat with Deena at lunch and told her we got a piece of mail with her address on it by mistake. All I had to do was ask what her mother's name was. She said Tracy, and I said, 'Nope. That's not the name on the letter.' And that was it. So easy I almost laughed."

"Good work, Tara. So, her name is Tracy Allen."

"Right." She sat up straighter. "Can we get started right now?"

As I tied the bow I said, "Sorry, kiddo, but I won't be able to work on it until after supper. I've got a lot of arrangements to finish before I head home, and then I'll have to make food. But I promise I'll work on it this evening."

"I'll do some research tonight, too. Call me as soon as you find something."

By five-thirty we had the workroom cleaned and prepped for the next day and were heading out the door. By five forty-five I was picking up a pizza I'd ordered and at six, Marco walked through the door to find a hot pizza and fresh green salad waiting for him.

"Delicious," Marco said, taking a bite of his pepperoni slice. "I'm famished." In between bites, he entertained our two pets weaving between his legs under the table.

"You're keeping me in suspense, Marco. What did you find out at Bass Lake?"

Marco wiped his mouth with a napkin. "That Frank Vesco was never there."

"Frank was never at the fishing lodge?"

Marco took another bite of pizza and chewed it. "Nope," he said at last. "The manager checked his log and had no record of Frank being there."

"Then Frank's sister was right to be concerned."

"Yes. However, I found out that Frank did have a reservation."

"At least we know he'd planned on going. What else did you find?"

Marco took another bite. "Sorry, babe. I'm starving." He chewed and swallowed, then washed it down with a drink of water. "The manager said the reservation was made last minute. It was only because he'd just had a cancellation that he was able to squeeze Frank in."

"Did he know Frank?"

"Yes. He remembered him and John. He also remembered that a woman who identified herself as Mr. Vesco's secretary made the reservation."

"Do you think that's legit?"

"Only one way to find out. Tomorrow I'll call Frank's office and ask her."

"Then what's our next step?"

"I'd like to talk to Frank's wife again and see if she can think of anyone else Frank might have gone fishing with. Maybe they had a last-minute change of plans."

"Wouldn't Frank have canceled his reservation at the fishing lodge?"

"Maybe his secretary was supposed to do that. I'll make it a point to ask her tomorrow." He took another bite then asked, "How was your day?"

I made a quick decision not to bring up Tara's investigation and instead told him about Jillian's donation and some of the stranger orders I'd had that day. We finished dinner, cleaned up the kitchen, and then Marco volunteered to take Seedy out for his evening walk. I was more than happy to let him do it. While he was out, I curled up on the sofa, opened my laptop, and began a search for Tracy Allen.

On Facebook, I found three Tracy Allens, but only one listed her hometown as New Chapel. I clicked on her name and saw that we had a friend in common, Barbara Ferrari. I didn't recognize the name, so I checked Barbara's page and found that she lived in New Chapel. She looked familiar with her short blond bob and thin rosy cheeks, but I couldn't place her. I typed the name Barbara Ferrari into my Notes app on my phone and moved on.

I scrolled through Tracy Allen's page. Her most recent post had been made a week before, a picture of her youngest daughter falling into a huge pile of leaves. There were many photos of both of her daughters, Deena and Joy. There was a picture of her husband with his arm around the girls, too, but none of the two adults together. Other than that, the remaining photos were either of flowers from her garden or dishes that she had cooked. It seemed she was a real homebody.

I found Tracy on Instagram, too, and as before, her last post had been a week earlier, with a caption that read Mom is doing much better! @AliceBailey. I tapped on her name and found out that Alice had recently undergone surgery.

"That could explain the trip to Colorado," I said out loud.

On Instagram I also found photos of Deena and Joy with their grandmother, taken, the caption said, in Indianapolis.

Wait. Was that where Alice Bailey lived?

I did a search for Alice Bailey on Facebook and found out that Indianapolis was correct. On Alice's page, I also found photos of her with her two daughters, Tracy Allen and Sheila Morris. I went back to Tracy's page and looked for a post that mentioned her sister Sheila. It took a long time to scroll back through her timeline, but it paid off. I finally found a post that listed Sheila's maiden name as Bailey, too. And lo and behold, on

Sheila's page, it listed her hometown as Indianapolis. Then who lived in Colorado?

"What are you working on?" Marco asked, leaning over my shoulder.

I tried to hide the fact that he'd startled me. "Just reading my Facebook posts."

"Who's Sheila Bailey?"

I could feel Marco staring at me. I rolled my head backward on the cushion to look at him. "Someone I met at Bloomers."

He smiled, but not in his sexy way where his mouth curled at the corner. This was a grin, a knowing grin where his eyes squinted just enough to see right through me.

"Okay, she's not someone I met at Bloomers. She's a relative of the people Tara is investigating."

"That *you* are now investigating."

"Yes, Marco, that *I* am now investigating." I huffed and shut the laptop.

Marco traced a line from my shoulder down to my hand. "You don't have to lie to me, you know."

"Well, you haven't been incredibly supportive lately."

He inhaled and sighed, then rounded the couch and sat next to me. "And what did my little sleuth learn?"

I gazed at him skeptically. "You're just going to shoot down my ideas."

"I won't."

"Okay. I learned that Tracy's mother and sister live in Indianapolis, and she doesn't mention any other close family members. So why is Deena's story that her mother went to Colorado?"

Marco touched his fingertip to my nose. "Maybe she has an aunt in Colorado. Or cousins. Maybe she's just never mentioned them on Facebook."

I could feel my face start to burn. "You're doing it."

"I'm sorry. I'll stop. Go ahead."

"Tracy posted that her mother had just had surgery and was recovering well. Now, would a daughter head out west while her mother was recuperating?"

"Didn't you say her sister lives in Indianapolis? Wouldn't she be the one to care for their mother?"

I stood up. "Marco, you are exasperating. Not everything can be explained away."

"But most things can."

"Yes, individually these instances can be easily explained, but when you add them all up . . . you know what? Forget it. I still say dragging something long and bulky out to a shed in the middle of the night needs investigating."

Marco watched me take the laptop over to the kitchen counter, then he said, "I'm sorry. I'm not trying to upset you. If you feel this strongly then you have my support. What's your next move?"

"I don't know. I'm going into the bedroom to call Tara."

Marco held up his hands, palms facing out. "Don't let me stop you."

I was still huffing when I sat down on my bed to call my niece.

"You sound funny," she said immediately.

"I'm fine. I just wanted to let you know what I found out."

"I'm all ears."

I gave her a detailed rundown of my findings along with Marco's logical explanations and let her draw her own conclusions.

"That confirms my information," Tara said. "I found out that Tracy Allen is supposedly on a church retreat, and she can't communicate with anyone. Her grandmother called while I was there, and she sounded concerned."

"Okay, then Tracy Allen is on a church retreat. That's one mystery solved."

"Not really," she said. "If it was just a simple church retreat, why would her grandmother be concerned? And why is Deena so reluctant to tell me where her mom is?"

"That sounds like a family issue, not a murder mystery."

"I think Deena's lying, Aunt Abby. I could hear it in her voice. Something is wrong. Maybe you could call her grandma and check the story, just to get an inside scoop."

Smoke jumped up on the bed and curled up beside me. As I stroked his soft, silver fur, I said, "I don't know, Tara. I think we should wait a few days to see if Mrs. Allen returns. If she doesn't, I'll have to make some calls, and you'll have to question Deena some more. Will you be up to it?"

"I'll find a way, don't worry."

"In the meantime, don't go snooping on your own."

She hesitated for a moment, then said with reluctance, "Okay."

CHAPTER EIGHT

TARA

I wasn't going to break my promise to Aunt Abby because I wasn't going to snoop on my own. David was coming with me.

I had already put my phone on silent and dressed in the darkest clothes I could find. I sat at my desk watching the backyard, making sure there was no activity before we snuck out, then looked down at my phone. Ten minutes past midnight. Where was he? I searched David's window, but the lights were off. Had he fallen asleep? My nervous excitement started to wane as I realized that without David, I couldn't get into the shed. He had the lock pick set.

My eyes suddenly felt heavy and I stifled a long yawn. I looked over at Seedling as he, too, yawned and stretched and gave me the sleepy puppy dog eyes. He had made himself cozy at the foot of my bed and rolled onto his back, waiting for my arrival. *Okay, puppy. Time for bed.*

Then I noticed a quick flash of light outside. I picked up the binoculars and focused on David's window, my excitement returning. After another quick flash, I heard my phone vibrate on the desk.

David: *Still spying on me?*

Tara: *Nope*

His bedroom light flashed again.

Tara: *I didn't see that.*

David: *Meet me by the woodpile.*

I snuck downstairs in my dark tennis shoes, dark blue jeans, and black hoodie, any stray noises masked by the hum of the furnace. I had already unlocked the back door before bed, and I was careful not to trigger the motion detector floodlights when I closed the door behind me. As I made my way across the yard, I noticed the leaves in Deena's yard hadn't been raked and every footfall was a crunching alarm announcing my every move. I had to be careful. David was already crouched behind the woodpile when I arrived. He was dressed in a black wool cap, dark gloves, and his bright green and white varsity jacket, making him easily visible in the dark.

"You look like a cat burglar," he joked. "Ready for this?"

I looked up at the Allen's windows. No movement. The family room was dark, too. "Let's go."

David crunched through the leaves and I stopped him, pushing my finger to my lips. "Go around the leaves," I whispered.

We made our way quietly to the front of the shed. A firm breeze blew through the backyard and I started to shiver as David unrolled the lock pick set. He must've noticed me rubbing my arms because he set the items down and pulled off his jacket.

"Here," he said. "You're going to freeze."

I almost forgot what we were doing as he wrapped me in his jacket. I pulled the collar up and smiled at him. "Thank you."

After a few minutes of trying, I could tell David was getting frustrated. He switched out various picks, trying different combinations, but nothing seemed to work. "This is way harder than it looks," he whispered.

I circled the shed while David continued to work on the lock. On the backside, I shined the light from my phone through the broken, boarded-up window. I could still make out the dark shadow of a black plastic bag, but now I could also see what looked like a dark stain on the wooden floorboards. "David, look."

He met me by the window and took my phone. "What am I looking at?"

"Does that look like blood to you?"

He angled the phone and shook his head. "Looks like an oil stain to me."

"David, that's blood. There's a dead body inside this shed."

"Wouldn't a dead body have a strong odor at this point? All I smell is gasoline."

"Maybe the gas is covering up the smell. Any luck with the lock?"

"No, it's impossible."

"Let me try."

David and I walked quietly to the front of the shed. The picks were tiny, and the moonlight was barely enough to see what I was doing, but I was determined to get inside. After several attempts, I could start to feel my bare fingers tingle in the cold air. Then I dropped a pick to the ground and started to look for it when a light came on behind us.

"Someone's coming," David whispered.

I grabbed the lock pick set and followed David around to the side of the shed. I could hear a door open and heavy footsteps through the leaves coming toward us. We moved further back, hiding behind the woodpile. My breathing was hurried. My heart was pounding. David put his arm around me as we knelt down.

He pulled me close to whisper, "Deena's dad?"

I nodded. I was sure it was him.

The padlock clicked open and once again I heard a long squeak as the shed door opened wide. A flashlight came shining through the slats in the wood. What was he doing in there?

"Let's get out of here," David whispered again.

"Wait." I put my hands on the cold bark and pulled myself up just a little. "I want to see what he does."

The flashlight stopped moving, but stayed on, keeping the shed lit up from the inside. For a while, all I could hear were the leaves rustling in the breeze. I looked at David and pressed my finger to my lips once again, then barely whispered, "I'm going to the window."

"Don't," David mouthed.

But I had already made up my mind. Standing, I planned out my path, each footstep between the leaves, and followed the path flawlessly, making no noise as I approached the window. I looked back at David. He raised himself from his crouched position to look over the woodpile, then lost his balance and reeled backward, crunching the leaves loudly behind him.

Instantly, the flashlight's beam inside the shed began to move. I froze in place. David quickly pulled himself up and motioned wildly for me to join him. I looked down at my path, retracing my steps until I was once again hidden behind the woodpile. David knelt beside me and we waited together in silence, hardly daring to breathe. After what seemed like an hour, I finally pulled myself up to see what was happening.

"Get down," David whispered.

The shed door creaked close. I folded myself into a tight ball, and David did the same as Deena's father walked around the corner of the shed and shined the light our way. As the beam swept across the woodpile, I felt as though any movement would give us away, any small amount of breath that escaped my lips would turn into a cloud of vapor above our heads, calling out our position. I thought for sure we were caught.

After a long pause, I could see the beam of light sweeping back and forth across the yard. Then I heard the padlock click and the crunch of leaves as Deena's father walked back toward the house. As the door closed behind him, I sagged back onto the cold ground, still shaking.

David's quiet laugh shook me from my fright. He leaned back on his elbows and turned his head to smile at me. "I thought we were caught for sure."

As though releasing the tension in my body, I couldn't help but laugh, too, but after a few seconds, the adrenaline started to wear off and I began to shiver again.

"What was Deena's dad doing out here at midnight?" David asked.

"I don't know, but he's up to something."

"Have you asked Deena about it?"

I shook my head.

"Why not?"

"What would I say? Is your father storing a dead body in the shed?"

"Yes!" he said insistently. "That's exactly what you say. And then you ask her to open the shed door."

"But what if her mom really is in there?"

"That's the point, right? That's what we're trying to find out."

"I can't ask her yet, not until we know for sure."

"Then I think we should call it a night."

"Wait a minute," I said as David began to put away his lock pick set. "Are you giving up already?"

"For tonight. Yes."

I stopped him from standing. "David, I dropped one of the picks in front of the shed. We need to get it before we leave."

"No way."

"Why?"

David looked at me. "Tara, he heard us. That's why he left. Whatever he was doing, we interrupted, and I'll bet he's inside right now watching the shed."

I sat for a moment, pulling the warm sleeves of David's jacket around my cold hands. Was he right? Looking up from the woodpile, I searched the Allen's windows. The only window I couldn't see was the family room, where I knew Mr. Allen would have a clear view of the shed. I looked back at David. "Well, do you believe me now?"

He breathed in and out deeply, shaking his head. "I don't know what I believe, but something shady is going on and I don't want to be caught out here."

"Just give me a minute," I said, removing David's bright varsity jacket and handing it to him. "I'm going to sneak around in the dark and look for the pick. I'll be almost invisible."

"You're going to get caught."

"No, I won't."

I felt the cold air wrap around me. The wind picked up a bit causing the branches to sway rhythmically in the trees overhead. Several leaves fell in my path as I rounded the front of the shed, getting down onto my hands and knees to peer around the corner.

The lights were off in the family room, of course, but my eyes had adjusted to the darkness. There didn't seem to be anyone standing at the windows, and even so, at that distance it would be hard to spot me as long as I moved slowly. I pulled the dark hood around my head and continued on all fours to the shed door. I searched the cold ground and pressed my hands in the blades of grass but found nothing. I knew it had been right there.

After a few more minutes of searching, I suddenly felt a sinking feeling in my stomach. What if Mr. Allen found the lock pick?

David wrapped his jacket around me when I knelt beside him. "Did you find it?"

I pulled the flaps around my sides, feeling the warmth once again. "No. I couldn't find it."

"What do we do now, Sherlock?"

"I don't know. Maybe it's just lost in the grass."

"Or maybe the wife killer found it."

"Even if he did, he can't trace it back to us."

"Then, are we done for the night?"

I didn't want to be done. Even though it was cold and late, even though Mr. Allen could be on his way back out to finish what he'd started, I didn't want the night to end, but I couldn't think of a reason to stay.

"Let's talk tomorrow, okay?" David asked.

"Okay."

"Goodnight, Tara."

There was an awkward moment where David reached toward me and I didn't know what to do. I took his outstretched hand, thinking maybe he wanted to kiss me.

He squeezed my hand. "Can I have my jacket back?"

CHAPTER NINE

ABBY

Friday

"We'd like to return this candle."

It was just after opening when I paused in stocking the display case and glanced around. A couple was standing in front of Lottie at the cash counter, the woman holding one of my mother's candles.

"Sure," Lottie said. "I'm sorry you didn't like it."

"Like it?" the man said. "Look at our eyes! They're still red and irritated and it's been two days. We lit the candle at suppertime and by bedtime, we could barely see!"

"I'm so sorry," Lottie said. She opened the cash drawer and drew out the money. "Here you go, and again, I apologize."

The man pocketed the money and they started toward the door where the woman paused to say, "You'd better warn your customers. Those candles are a danger."

As the customers reached for the handle, the front door opened, and Rosa stepped inside. She wore a bold black-and-white top with a short skirt and thick, black oversized sunglasses. She held the door for the angry customers and apologized to me for being late. I hadn't even had time to ask why before she ducked into the workroom.

I joined Lottie at the counter to see which candle had been returned, but the packaging was off. I took a sniff. "Wow, that's strong." I sniffed it again. "That must be the curry candle. I didn't notice how powerful the smell was before it was lit."

"I hope it's just an aberration, sweetie," Lottie said, "or we'll have other customers coming in to complain. You'll have to tell your mother."

I checked the three candles left on the oak table and saw that there was still one remaining New Delhi Curry Candle. Had there been more sold? I crossed my fingers and hoped that the candles that had been sold were not infused with the same strong spice.

After stocking the display case with dark red roses and bright orange mums, I went through the purple curtain into the workroom where Rosa was making an all-white arrangement. "That's beautiful, Rosa."

"Gracias." She turned the arrangement toward me, and I noticed she was still wearing the oversized pair of sunglasses.

"What's wrong? Too bright in here?"

She pulled the glasses from her face, and I was taken back by her bright-red bloodshot eyes.

"Oh my God, don't tell me."

"*Sí.* The Mexican Spice."

I hurried back out onto the sales floor and removed all of the candles with spice in the name.

✿❀✿

Mid-morning, Marco called to update me. "I just got off the phone with Frank's secretary and she confirmed that she had indeed made the reservation at the fishing lodge. She said it was a last-minute trip."

"Is that normal?"

"She seemed to think so. And Eileen Vesco couldn't think of anyone else Frank might have gone fishing with. She said all he told her was that he wanted to get away from it all. She said it wouldn't have been unusual for him to go alone."

"I sure didn't get that feeling from Frank's friend John."

"I didn't either. Eileen did express surprise that I was still investigating. She said she thought it was a waste of time. I told her Frank hadn't been to the fishing lodge, and she said there was another place he liked to go, kind of off the grid. She said it was in the same vicinity as the lodge but was just a cabin near a lake."

"And she had no way of getting a hold of her husband?"

"She said she texted him after we'd been there and got a text back saying that he was doing fine. And that was apparently all she needed to know."

"Marco, why is Eileen the only person getting messages from Frank?"

"I don't know, but as long as Eileen is fine with his absence, there's nothing we can do. We don't have any way of knowing where he is and there's no trail to follow. We're just going to have to wait until Saturday and see if Frank returns. His sister is supposed to let me know."

"Okay, but I don't have a good feeling about it."

"Let's hope you're wrong."

At three-thirty my mom popped through the purple curtain with a cardboard box full of candles and a big smile. "Only three dinner candles left!"

"I know," I said. "Congratulations. But there's something I need to tell you."

"Yes, congratulations, Maureen," Rosa said as she scrambled to put on her sunglasses.

"It's about the candles, Mom," I started.

"Yes," Rosa interrupted. She clapped her hands together. "They are a success!"

I was thoroughly confused. Rosa looked at me through her dark glasses and even though I couldn't see her eyes, I got the hint. I didn't say another word about it.

My mom looked pleased. "I'm glad you like them, Rosa." She looked through the box. "I have a new scent, this one in honor of your homeland. I call it Columbian Zest. I want you to have one. No charge."

"Gracias, Maureen," Rosa gushed, accepting the deep red candle. "I can't wait to smell it."

"I brought a book of matches," Mom said. "You can smell it right now."

Rosa's smile froze in place.

Mom dug through her purse. "I figured the candle might sell better if we light one on the sales floor."

"No!" Rosa and I called out at the same time.

My mom looked at us in surprise. "No?"

"What I mean is," I said, "we wouldn't want to spoil the customer's surprise of smelling the scent at home."

"Abby, I have one for you and Marco, too. I call it, Forty-Six Shades of Green. It's an Irish candle."

"Thanks, Mom." I took the candle and gave her a hug. "I'll try it out at dinner tonight."

I turned to Rosa after my mom left the shop. "What was that all about?"

She took off the glasses and rubbed the corner of her eye. "I cannot stand to break your mother's heart."

"She's going to keep making them," I told her. "Someone could sue us."

"Then we'll take the candles and hide them in the basement."

Rosa and I gathered the remaining candles and took them through the workroom and kitchen to the steep flight of stairs that led to the basement. Downstairs, we passed shelves containing remnants of my mother's failed art projects and hid the candles in the back corner behind of box of old receipts.

Rosa turned to me with red-rimmed eyes. "We will never speak of this again."

TARA

"You snuck over there at midnight?" Aunt Abby asked, clearly not happy with me. "I told you not to go over there."

My mom walked by my room, so I pulled the phone tighter against my ear and almost whispered. "You're missing the point. Mr. Allen came out to the tool shed to do something – we couldn't tell what it was - but when he heard a noise, he freaked out and went back inside. That was at midnight, Aunt Abby! Midnight!"

There was silence on the other end for a moment, as though she was pondering my revelation, then she said, "You promised me you wouldn't go snooping over there. What if you'd been caught? What if he really does have a dead body in that shed? That's irresponsible and dangerous."

"Then you think there's a body in there, too."

"That's not what I'm saying, Tara, but I do think something is off at that house. My inner radar is pinging."

"That's what I've been trying to tell you!" I said. "Mine has been going off for the whole week."

"Okay, here's what I'm going to do. I'm going to contact Mrs. Allen's friend from Facebook and see if she'll talk to me. Maybe she knows what's going on."

"Good. Oh. And one other thing, Auntie A. My mom and dad are leaving for their anniversary cruise on Saturday. Can you come over and stay with me until the end of the week? I was supposed to stay with Aunt Portia and Uncle Jonathan, but now with everything going on with Deena, I don't want to leave my house."

Aunt Abby took her time answering. What I didn't tell her was that I'd already told my parent's that she would stay with me. "You only have to stay at night," I added.

"How many nights?"

"Just until next Saturday," I told her. "And we could keep our eye on Mr. Allen. We might even catch him sneaking out to the shed again. Please, Aunt Abby?"

I could hear a reluctant sigh, but I took it as a good sign. "Marco could come over, too. And you could bring Seedy!"

"Okay, I'll stay with you, but on one very important condition."

"Anything. I promise."

"No more sneaking out to the neighbor's yard."

This time I was the one that took my time answering. "Okay, Auntie A."

ABBY

As soon as I got off the phone with my niece, I finished the floral arrangement I'd been working on, then sat down at the computer and logged onto Facebook. I found the name of Tracy Allen's friend Barbara Ferrari in my Notes app on my phone and went to her Facebook page. Using Barbara's contact information, I gave her a call.

"Ms. Ferrari, this is Abby Knight Salvare from the Salvare Detective Agency. Do you have a minute to talk?"

"Yes," she said hesitantly.

"We have a client who is concerned about the whereabouts of Tracy Allen and we were wondering if you knew where she was."

"Who's your client?"

"All I can tell you is that it's someone close to her."

"Honestly, I've been wondering about Tracy, too. All she said to me was that she was going away for a few days, but she hasn't responded to any of my text messages and she hasn't posted anything on Facebook or Instagram."

"Did she mention anything to you about visiting family in Colorado?"

"I wasn't aware that she had family in Colorado. I thought they were all in Indiana."

"How about a religious retreat?"

"A retreat in Colorado?" She thought for a moment. "I guess it's possible. Maybe I'll give Deena a call and see if she knows anything."

"If you do, please don't mention that we spoke."

"Why?"

"We don't want to upset her if it's just a false alarm."

"I see. Okay."

"Thank you for the help, Ms. Ferrari."

I ended the call and sat there thinking about Tracy Allen and the fact that she hadn't told her best friend where she was going. Had she told her mother? I pulled up Alice Bailey's Facebook page and looked for her contact information.

It took about ten minutes to find Alice's telephone number using Marco's go-to search engine. I called and after three rings a woman picked up.

"Mrs. Bailey, this is Abby Salvare of the Salvare Detective Agency. We have a client who is concerned about the whereabouts of your daughter Tracy. Do you have any information I can pass along?"

"Detective agency?"

"Yes. Salvare Detective Agency."

"I've never heard of you, young lady, and I'm not about to give out personal information to a stranger. Goodbye."

"Please, Mrs. Bailey, check out our website and you'll see that we're a legitimate business. We have a client who's worried that something happened to Tracy, and we'd like to make sure she's safe. Let me give you our website address and I'll wait while you check it out."

She heaved a sigh. "Hold on then."

I gave her our web address and waited. She came back on the line a few minutes later to say, "Okay, I believe you, but I can't help you. My daughter is unreachable at the moment."

"Are you aware that she's been unreachable all week?"

"Yes." There was a long pause. "I'm concerned about Tracy, too. I'd invited her to visit before my surgery, but she never showed up. My granddaughter told me she was on a church retreat, but I wasn't aware she'd joined a church."

"Is her husband part of this church?"

"I have no idea. I've tried to contact him, but he hasn't returned my phone calls. I don't know what to do."

"Mrs. Bailey, are you aware that you can request that the local police do a wellness check on your daughter? They might be able to get some answers."

"I wasn't aware of that, but maybe that's the thing to do. Thank you, Abby."

"And thank you, Mrs. Bailey, for talking to me."

I hung up and double-checked Tracy's social media accounts. There was no mention of any involvement with a religious group. Could Mr. Allen have made up the church retreat story as a cover for his missing wife?

And who was Mr. Allen anyway?

I returned to Tracy's Facebook page and read her bio. She reported that she'd been married to Dr. Paul Allen for twenty years. He was a doctor?

Paul Allen didn't have either a Facebook or Instagram page, but I did find his website listing him as a psychologist and marriage counselor, which seemed quite ironic. There was an entire page of testimonials, so it appeared he knew his stuff.

Our business phone line rang, jerking me back to the present. With a spindle full of orders and more coming in, I had to get back to work.

TARA

I sat at my desk that evening staring down at my history exam. What was I going to tell my parents? I had never done so poorly on an exam, and even though I hadn't failed, the grade I'd received was barely passing. Maybe I was spending too much time spying on the neighbors. Maybe I'd gotten too carried away with my murder mystery. Even David had received a better grade than me. I looked at the binoculars sitting on my desk and sighed. Time to get back to reality. I put the binoculars on the floor by my feet and pulled my geometry book from my bookbag.

Fifteen minutes later, I was using the protractor to work out a problem when I saw red and blue flashing lights across our two yards. It appeared to be coming from the front of the Allen's house. I grabbed the binoculars from the floor and put them to my eyes just in time to see two police officers enter the family room. Had they found out something about Deena's mom?

I focused on Deena's window where I could see her standing in her doorway rubbing her arms, as though chilled. Her little sister came up to her and Deena put her arm around her and ushered her into her room, where they sat on the bed together talking.

I picked up my phone and called my aunt. "Guess what just happened? The police went to the Allen's house! What do you suppose that was about?"

"Calm down, Tara," she said. "I called Deena's grandmother this afternoon and found out she's concerned about Tracy, too. I suggested she have the police do a wellness check."

"But why would they show up with flashing lights?"

"I don't know, but as long as you're on the phone, I also talked to Tracy's best friend and learned that she thinks it's strange Tracy hasn't called her or posted anything all week. So that makes two people who are concerned."

"What do we do now?"

"Let's see if the police visit shakes things up a bit. Maybe she'll return home."

"I'm tired of waiting, Aunt Abby."

"For now, that's all we can do."

I hung up and returned to my desk, where I should've finished my geometry assignment. Instead, I sat there with the binoculars glued to my eyes watching the window across from me.

In the middle of the night, I was awakened by a creaking sound. I sat up in bed and flung the covers off. I knew that sound!

At the window, I pulled back one side of my curtains, grabbed the binoculars, and focused them on the yard below. By the moonlight, I could see that the shed door was standing open. I waited at the window until my arms got tired and began to wonder if the door had blown open. But that wouldn't have happened if the shed were locked.

And then I saw a big figure backing away from the shed dragging something long and bulky, just like I'd seen before. The figure had to be Mr. Allen. But this time he was taking his bulky load away from the shed. He dragged it around the side of the house and disappeared from sight. Five minutes later, I saw the Allen's silver SUV drive away from their house.

Had he just moved his wife's body?

CHAPTER TEN

ABBY

Saturday

Saturday morning started with an appointment for a mother and her daughter to choose flowers for the daughter's December wedding. I seated them in the coffee and tea parlor, fixed them up with cups of tea and the wedding planner catalog, and sat down opposite them.

"What did you have in mind?" I asked the bride.

"We'd like something traditional," the mother answered, "a Christmas theme with lots of red."

"No," the bride-to-be said, "*you'd* like something traditional. I want a contemporary wedding, and that doesn't mean all *Christmasy.* I think white would be nice."

"White!" The mother stared at her in horror. "White? For the holidays?"

"Mother, it isn't about the holidays. It's about my wedding, and I want white."

The two women glared at each other until Grace came up to our table and placed a plate of scones in the center, along with a bowl of clotted cream.

"What's this?" the mother asked, looking at me as though I was trying to pull something.

"These are almond scones, with our compliments," I said, and daintily picked one up. "Grace makes them every morning. Try one."

The daughter immediately chose one and broke off the end. She popped it in her mouth, closed her eyes, and chewed slowly. "Yum," she said. "These are heavenly. Mummy, try one."

Her mother took a bite and sighed with pleasure. "These *are* heavenly. They remind me of the pastries your grandmother made. Do you remember them?"

The daughter smiled at her mother. "I do. Grandma would give me a big glass of milk to go with them." She sighed. "I miss Grandma."

The two women gazed at each other with smiles, until finally, the mother said, "So you want all white flowers."

The daughter nodded, her mouth full.

"How about white with touches of red? It was your grandmother's favorite color," her mother asked and took another bite of scone.

The daughter chewed thoughtfully for a moment, then reached across the table and put her hand atop her mother's. "I think that would be nice."

I glanced over at Grace. She winked.

I was back in the workroom a short time later when Tara's name popped up on my phone. "What's up?" I asked.

"You'll never guess what happened," she said with excitement. "In the middle of the night, Mr. Allen dragged that long, bulky thing out of his shed, loaded it in his car, and drove away!"

"You could see that from your window?"

"Yes! I saw him drag the body out front, and then a little bit later, I saw their SUV drive away. At three-thirty a.m. I'll bet the police visit scared him so bad, he had to get his wife's body out of the shed. We have to do something!"

"Okay, let me think. Today is Saturday. Let's see if Mrs. Allen comes back today."

"Trust me. She's not coming back. We need a plan."

"First things first. We wait to see if Mrs. Allen comes back. I'll be over tonight around seven. We can come up with a plan then."

Rosa and I worked all through the morning. I went out to the sales floor to help customers when Lottie had left to make deliveries. Shortly before noon, Lottie returned, so I headed back to the workroom where I found Rosa trimming blue delphiniums. On the table near her lay a pile of blue scabious, bluebells, and blue phlox.

"That's going to be beautiful, Rosa."

"Gracias. It's for a fortieth birthday. The wife, she told me she wanted something *especial* for her husband, so I suggested everything in blue."

"He'll love it."

I was about to pull an order from the spindle when my cell phone dinged again. I'd left it sitting on the desk next to the computer and when I went to pick it up, I saw Marco's name on the screen. "Hello, handsome. What's going on?"

"Hey, beautiful, I've got some bad news."

I instantly had a sick feeling in the pit of my stomach. "What happened?"

"The police have a body in the morgue that they've identified as Frank Vesco's. His body was found near the Bass Lake fishing lodge this morning."

"Oh, no. How did you find out?"

"Sean just called with the news."

Thank God for Sgt. Sean Reilly. My dad had worked with him before he'd left the force, and Marco had trained with him after he'd left the Army Rangers. Reilly had come through for us in our investigations many times, and although it turned out that Marco hadn't liked the police force – the red tape too restricting – his friendship with Reilly had lasted. And now with our private investigation business, Reilly's help was invaluable.

"Hikers were walking through a wooded area and saw a body on the ground. The police are calling it an apparent suicide."

"How can they be sure?"

"Sean said he saw crime scene photos. There appears to be a gunshot wound through the right temple. A suicide note was found next to the body and a gun was still clutched in Frank's hand."

"How did they know it was Frank? Was his ID on his body?"

"Yes. His wallet was in his pocket. His cell phone was in his shirt pocket."

"I guess that ends the missing person's case."

"I guess so," Marco said. "I'm sure Sylvie will be calling with the news."

"Poor Sylvie. What an awful way to lose her twin."

After I'd hung up with Marco, I studied the order I'd pulled and walked to the big cooler to choose my stems, but my mind was still on the startling news. What in Frank's life had made him kill himself? Could marital problems be the cause? Had there been any problems with his business? Who could we talk to? How could we get more answers? Would his friend John have an idea of why it'd happened?

Okay, Abby, stop. What had happened was none of my business now. I pushed the sad news to the back of my mind and forced myself to continue working.

By mid-afternoon, Jillian popped through the curtain singing, "Break time. I told Grace to bring us some coffee." She slid onto a wooden stool across from me.

I trimmed another yellow mum and placed it in the vase. "Sorry, Jill. I don't have time to stop right now. How are you doing with your six-piece clothing challenge?"

She slid out of her green swing coat to model her outfit. "This is my fourth day. So far so good."

"You look very nice, Jillian," Rosa said. "I don't know how you're doing it. I'd be sick of my six pieces by now."

Jillian ran her fingers through her long coppery locks. "No. Not sick of them yet."

She didn't look so sure.

"By the way," she said, "did Grace take all of my donations to the shelter?"

I turned the vase to see the other side. "Two days ago. Why?"

"Just wondering."

As though she'd been standing on the other side listening, Grace chose that moment to step through the curtain with a smile aimed at Jillian. "I thought I saw you come in, love. I just want you to know that the women were so excited to have your donations. It meant a lot to them."

"That's great news." Jillian beamed with pride. "What else did they say?"

Grace paused. "That's all, dear. They were very excited."

Lottie came in through the back, having just returned from making deliveries. "Here you are again," she said to Jillian.

I glanced from her to my cousin. "Again?"

"Yes," Lottie said. "I saw Jillian standing outside Windows on the Square staring through the window at the mannequins."

Jillian fingered a lock of hair. "I was just checking out their outfits."

She'd never last two more days.

I was in Bloomer's parlor eating a sandwich when my cell phone rang, and Marco's name popped up. "Hey, Sunshine, how's it going?"

"I was just grabbing a quick bite. What's up?"

"Our case isn't over. Sylvie Freeman just called. She's extremely upset and said there was no way her brother would've killed himself. She'd like to meet with us as soon as possible. Are you busy?"

I looked at the spindle and saw that the orders had dwindled. Then I spied the extra flowers from a floral arrangement I'd just finished. "Pick me up in five minutes."

I worked quickly, putting together a beautiful bouquet for Sylvie. I let my assistants know I wouldn't be gone long and met Marco at the curb.

When Sylvie Freeman met us at the door, her eyes were swollen and red and she held a tissue to her nose. "Are those for me?"

"We're so sorry, Mrs. Freeman," I said, handing over the bouquet as we stood in her small entrance hall.

Tears welled in her eyes. "They're lovely. Thank you."

She led us into her living room where we sank into an overstuffed blue sofa. There were two matching chairs opposite the sofa with a square, oak coffee table in the center. Framed photographs filled the walls between the long, double-hung windows, and ceramic angels of every size sat on the end tables.

"I appreciate your coming over so quickly." She paused to blot the tears that had fallen down her cheeks. "I know my brother, Mr. Salvare. He wouldn't have killed himself." She stopped when her lower lip trembled. She took a deep breath and went on. "Someone wrote that suicide note and staged that scene to make it look like he did it, but I know the truth. He was murdered."

"Did you tell that to the police?" Marco asked.

"Yes. I even demanded to see Frank's note. I told them I'd know whether it was genuine or not, but they brushed me off. They said Frank's wife would be handling matters, that it was her responsibility, not mine. So I'm out of the picture. But I'm not helpless. Not by a longshot. I want you to find the person who ended my brother's life."

"Then let's plunge right into our investigation," Marco said, as I took out the notebook and pen. "Let's start with the people closest to Frank."

"That would be his wife, Eileen, and his best friend, John."

"Anyone else? Any other close friends or family members?"

"Frank was close to his nephew Michael. They worked together."

"As I told you earlier," Marco said, "we did speak with Michael. We were surprised to learn that Frank was leaving his accounting business to him."

Sylvie's eyes widened in surprise. "Frank never told me that. I assumed Eileen would get it." She looked down, as though thinking, then said, "Let me tell you something about Michael. He's an extremely ambitious young man. And he would know Frank's handwriting well enough to mimic it."

"Then you think he should be investigated?" Marco asked.

"Yes, he definitely needs to be investigated." Sylvie paused again to wipe her eyes. "Michael isn't our nephew by blood, Mr. Salvare. He's Eileen's nephew."

I wrote it down. "What do you think about Frank's friend John?" I asked.

"A nicer man you'll never meet," Sylvie said. "He and Frank are – God help me, *were* – like brothers." She welled up again and turned away to wipe her eyes and collect herself. "I'm sorry. The news is still so fresh. What will I do without him?"

"Take your time," I said.

Sylvie shook her head. "Frank was a very private person. He didn't even like opening up to me, but he was a kind man. Devoted. Who could've done this?"

"Let me read the list," I said. "His wife Eileen. His friend John. His nephew by marriage Michael."

"That's all I can think of, but you might want to talk to Frank's secretary. She handled all of his business dealings, made his appointments, all of that. She would know more than me."

"I'll look into it," Marco said.

"Thank you for taking the time to investigate everyone." She looked at Marco. "But I know Eileen had something to do with this. I just know it."

"We're going to shake the bushes, Mrs. Freeman, and see what falls out," he said. "We'll keep you informed."

Back in the car, I buckled my seatbelt and said, "It looks like we have two strong suspects. Eileen Vesco, and Michael Porter, all in the family. What's our plan?"

"I'll try to contact Frank's secretary this afternoon, and first thing tomorrow morning I'm going to call Eileen Vesco again."

"Marco, her husband just died, and she might be responsible. I doubt she'll want to see us."

"Why don't you make an arrangement like you did for Sylvie. We can bring it to her and try to ask a few questions.

CHAPTER ELEVEN

TARA

"She wants me to wait and see if Deena's mother comes home."

"Then you should probably wait."

I was seated upright on my bed with Seedling curled up next to my pillow. The window was opened a crack letting in the cool Saturday afternoon breeze. I laid back with my phone to my ear, put my arm around Seedy, and sighed. "David, listen to me. There is no way I'm going to let this go, not until I find out what was in that shed."

"Isn't your aunt like a famous detective? You should listen to her. You don't have to let it go, just give it time."

"What if we don't have time? If there's evidence in that shed, then every second counts."

"Just watch, you're going to break into that shed and find nothing. He was probably hauling away a big bag of leaves or an old carpet. And then you're going to get caught and I'm going to tease you forever."

"I hate you."

"No, you don't."

I immediately blushed and fell silent. I still couldn't believe how casually David and I were talking now, and whether I wanted to admit it or not, that was mostly the reason I didn't want to wait. What would we talk about then? Would he still want to talk to me?

"Have you asked Deena about the shed?"

"No. I tried asking about her mother, but she made up some story about visiting family in Colorado. This is driving me crazy. I need to know what was inside that stupid shed."

"Tara, just wait a few days. Neither one of us can pick a lock and there's no way we could bust open that window without making noise."

"There's another way in," I told him. "I saw the spare shed key in the Allen's house by the back door. If I could get in there and grab that key, we could get inside."

"Wow, that seems a bit illegal."

"I'd give the key back. No one will ever know. I just need a reason to get back into Deena's house without raising suspicion."

"And how would you do that?"

"I could bring her something. A cake or something."

He laughed. "You're going to bake her a cake?"

"Or cookies . . . or . . ." I suddenly thought of the perfect idea.

"Or what?"

"David, what are you doing right now?"

"Nothing. Why?"

"Want to come over and bake some brownies?"

ABBY

"Did you talk to Frank's secretary already?" I asked, having just placed the yellow apron back over my head.

"Luckily, the business is open half a day on Saturdays. She didn't feel comfortable giving me any personal details, but she agreed that something doesn't feel right about Frank's death. She verified that Michael would inherit the accounting business, and she said that Frank had taken out a substantial life insurance policy almost one year ago to the day, with Eileen as the beneficiary. I checked into it and learned that insurance companies will pay benefits as long as it's been over a year since the policy was instituted."

"Eileen is involved in this, Marco, I'm sure of it."

"I agree. I tried calling her but she's not answering."

"What are we going to do?"

"Let's pay her a surprise visit this evening. In the meantime, I called Michael and he's going to meet us at the bar at four o'clock today. I know Bloomers closes early on Saturdays so I thought you could make it."

"We're swamped with funeral orders, but I should be done by four."

"Then let's meet at Down the Hatch at four o'clock."

Down the Hatch Bar and Grill was the town's local watering hole, a meeting place for the judges and attorneys from the courthouse across the street, a gathering place for the college students who attended New Chapel University, and a suppertime hang out for a group of active senior citizens. Decorated in a corny fishing theme, complete with a fake carp mounted above the long, dark wood bar, a bright blue plastic anchor on the wall above the row of booths opposite the bar, a big brass bell near the cash register, and a fisherman's net hanging from the beamed ceiling, it practically screamed for a rehab. Unfortunately, the patrons loved the old look, so Marco was hesitant to change it. I just had to look the other way.

The bar was already crowded when I walked in, the TV mounted above the bar showing a college football game. Through the dim light, I saw Marco standing behind the long, polished wood bar pouring a glass of wine, one of three bartenders working on a busy Saturday. He raised his hand to let me know he saw me and motioned with his head toward our booth, the last booth in the long row against the opposite wall. I sidled past a group of college kids standing at the bar talking and laughing and made my way to the booth.

"Here you go," my hubby said and placed the wine in front of me. "Michael just came in. I'll find out what he'd like to drink and send him back here."

I took a sip of my cabernet and looked up as a handsome young man in a neatly tailored gray suit making his way toward me. He stopped to talk to Marco before continuing.

"Hello," he said with a smile, sliding onto the bench seat across from me.

"Michael, I'm so sorry about your uncle."

As though he'd just remembered, he immediately sobered. "Thank you. It was quite a shock."

"How did you hear?"

"My aunt Eileen phoned me." He paused as Marco set a beer in front of him.

"We're so sorry," Marco said, sliding in beside me.

Michael shook his head. "I still can't believe he took his own life. It doesn't make sense. Business has been good. He seemed fine, happy to be going fishing . . ."

"What about on the home front?" Marco asked. "Any troubles there that you knew of?"

"Not that I ever heard about, but Uncle Frank never shared anything personal with me."

"When was the last time you talked to Frank?" Marco asked.

"The day before he left for his trip. But I received a text message from him saying that he was staying an extra few days."

"What day did you receive the message?" Marco asked.

"Let's see." He paused to think. "I talked to you on Tuesday, so it was Wednesday."

"Is that all it said? Nothing about how he was feeling?"

"No. It was short and sweet."

I wrote it down.

"Michael," Marco began, "Frank's sister doesn't believe he took his own life. She thinks someone else had a hand in it."

Michael was in the middle of sipping his beer and set it down quickly. "She thinks he was murdered?"

"She said there was no reason for him to take his own life."

"Maybe so, but I can't think of anyone who would've wanted him dead. Everyone liked Uncle Frank."

"Are you aware that your Aunt Eileen will receive the life insurance payout from your Uncle's death?"

"So? That's normal, isn't it?"

"She took out the policy one year ago, almost to the day. The insurance company does not pay out until after a year."

"You think Aunt Eileen killed Frank?"

"That's what I'm asking you," Marco said. "Do you have any reason to believe your Aunt would need the insurance money?"

"I find that hard to believe," Michael answered. "Not Aunt Eileen. The only person with money issues that I know of is Aunt Sylvie. She was supposed to live off her family's inheritance but I'm always finding records of Frank loaning money to her."

I wrote down *Sylvie money issues?*

"What will happen to the accounting business now?" Marco asked.

"I plan to close it until after the funeral."

"Has a date been set?"

"Yes. Visitation will be Sunday afternoon – tomorrow - and the funeral will be on Monday."

"Thanks," Marco said, as I jotted it down.

Michael stayed another ten minutes, sharing stories about his uncle with Marco, while I sipped my wine and watched him. I wasn't getting a bad vibe from Michael. I wondered whether Marco felt the same way.

"I've got an hour," Marco told me after Michael had left. "Let's pick up your floral arrangement and drop by Eileen Vesco's."

While Marco went to get his car from the parking lot on the street behind Down the Hatch, I dashed back to Bloomers and pulled the condolence arrangement from the big cooler. I met Marco out front and held the wrapped vase of flowers in my lap on the ride to Eileen's house.

"What did you think of our meeting with Michael?" Marco asked.

"He seemed straightforward with his answers, just a nice young man who inherited a business. I didn't sense anything sinister like Sylvie seemed to hint at. How about you?"

"Nothing other than that he didn't seem too shaken up about Frank's death."

"Inheriting the business is a windfall for him, Marco. Maybe he's still in shock over that. Or maybe Frank's passing just hasn't sunken in yet."

"Then you're not putting him at the top of the suspect list?"

"Absolutely not. Eileen is still number one."

Marco's phone rang. He handed it to me, and I saw Sgt. Reilly's name on the screen. "It's Reilly," I whispered to Marco, then answered, "Hey, Sarge. It's Abby. Marco's driving."

"I won't keep you long," he said. "I just wanted to let Marco know that the coroner said the body's state of decomposition indicated that it had been cold for at least a week."

"Wow. I'll let Marco know."

"But the forensics found something extremely odd," Reilly added. "There was no blood at the scene."

At the news, I pushed the speakerphone button so Marco could hear. "No blood from the gunshot wound?" I asked.

"There was blood on his body and clothes, but none at the crime scene, which indicates his body was moved."

"Which also means he didn't kill himself."

"That's how it looks," Reilly said.

Marco chimed in, "Can you get a copy of the suicide note?"

"I shouldn't have a problem with that," he said quietly, as though someone was listening. "I'll have to find the right time."

I gave Marco a thumbs up. "Thanks, Sarge."

I ended the call and dropped the phone in the cupholder. "Why do you want a copy of the suicide note?"

"Because I have a plan. We go to Frank's viewing and take a photo of the signatures in the guest book. Hopefully, both Eileen and Michael will have signed it. Then we compare their signatures with the suicide note. I think there'll be enough handwriting to at least rule them out."

"Good plan. Now let me tell you what Reilly said."

"Go ahead."

"He said Frank had been dead at least a week before he was found. So that means that he died soon after Eileen Vesco got a text from him saying that all was well. Does that make sense?"

"No, it doesn't. And something else isn't adding up, Abby. Both Michael and Eileen said that they heard from him on Wednesday. That was three days ago. He couldn't have texted." Marco pulled up in front of Eileen Vesco's house and shut off the engine. "Someone was using his phone."

Marco and I walked up the four steps to the porch of the Craftsman style home and rang the doorbell. A minute later, Eileen answered the door wearing a pink terrycloth bathrobe and white slippers. She had on a full face of makeup and her dark hair was pulled into a bun. She looked surprised when she saw the flowers.

"These are for you," I said as I handed her the arrangement, "with our condolences."

"Thank you. That's very kind of you."

"We know this is a difficult time for you," Marco said, "but do you have a few minutes to talk to us?"

Her features stiffened with displeasure. She set the vase on the floor behind her and turned back to say sharply, "I think we can safely assume my husband is no longer missing."

"Actually," I said, "that's not why we're here. Mrs. Freeman believes there's been foul play. And according to what we've just learned from the police—"

"I'll thank you to take Sylvie's crazy theory elsewhere. In case you've forgotten, I'm in mourning."

She stepped back and shut the door in our faces.

"That went well," I said as we started for the car. "She didn't even let me finish my sentence."

Marco was quiet until he opened my car door for me, then he said, "Don't you think a normal wife would've been curious about what we learned from the police?"

"Maybe she already knows."

Marco's forehead wrinkled as he closed my door and went around to the other side. After he slid in and started the motor, he turned to me. "If you were in Eileen's shoes and had just learned your husband committed suicide a week earlier, wouldn't you be wondering how he'd sent a text message to you just days ago? Wouldn't you agree with your sister-in-law that something was wrong?"

"You bet."

Marco grabbed my knee and squeezed. "I think you were right about our number one suspect." He pointed toward Eileen's house. "And here she is now."

I turned to look and saw her garage door lifting. We watched as she backed out and took off.

"That was fast," I said. "She must've gotten dressed very quickly."

Marco put the Prius in gear. "Let's see where she goes."

Staying well behind her, we followed Eileen across town to a business section of the downtown. Marco pulled over onto a cross street and we watched Eileen pull into a business complex. She exited her car wearing a long black coat and disappeared inside a low, flat brick building. We pulled into the empty parking lot far away from Eileen's car. The tall sign near the entrance listed a multitude of names and businesses.

"Where do you think she went?"

Marco scratched his chin. "It could be any one of these offices, but nothing seems to be open."

After fifteen minutes of waiting, Marco checked his watch and then put the car in drive. "I've got to get back to the bar."

"And I'm going to Tara's house this evening, don't forget. I'll take Seedy with me so she can play with Seedling."

TARA

At six o'clock, I stood outside Deena's backdoor and waited for her. I had texted her five minutes earlier and told her to meet me for a surprise.

The door opened and Deena stared at the outstretched plate in my hands. "You brought brownies?"

"Which I made, by the way." I smiled. "I saw you eating brownies at lunch, so I thought you might like some homemade."

She looked from me to the plate of brownies. "Okay. Come in, I guess."

I stepped inside and was struck again by how clean the kitchen looked, as though it was a showroom, not a real home. That's when I noticed a cross hanging above the kitchen sink.

"Let me get some paper plates," she said, "and we can take them to my room."

As soon as she went around the corner into the kitchen, I snatched the shed key off one of the pegs by the door and stuffed it in my jacket pocket. Above the row of keys was another cross. Had that been there before?

When I walked into the kitchen Deena had her back to me, pulling out paper plates from a cabinet. "I'll bet Joy would like a brownie," she said.

As we proceeded up the hallway to the stairs, I glanced into the living room. Mr. Allen wasn't there, but there was another cross hanging above the archway.

Upstairs, Deena led me into her room and called for her sister.

"Brownies!" Joy exclaimed in delight.

I dished one out onto a plate and handed it to her. "Homemade," I said. "Well, from a box mix."

Joy bit into one and sighed. "Yummy."

"Here you go," I said, and handed a plate to Deena.

I slid one onto my plate and bit into it, watching the sisters devour their brownies. Poor girls. They seemed so happy now. How long would it be before they found out that their mom was dead?

"Anyone for seconds?" I asked and turned toward the desk where I'd set the plate.

"Deena, we need to start packing," I heard a woman say.

"Okay, Mom."

Wait. What?

I swung around to find Deena's mom standing in the doorway. She was exactly as I'd remembered her with long, dark brown hair curled at the sides like Deena. Her smile was pleasant and she was wearing a large gold cross around her neck.

You could have knocked me over with a feather.

"You must be Tara," she said, walking into the room. "I'm Deena's mother."

For so long I'd been certain that Deena's mother was dead, that her father had killed her, I couldn't shake the feeling that I was meeting a ghost. "Tara Knight," I said with a catch in my throat. "Nice to meet you."

Deena's father walked by the room next. He didn't seem as calm as the rest of the family. "Time for your friend to leave, Dee. We have to go."

Deena didn't answer her father. She just rolled her eyes and told me she was sorry.

When the hallway had cleared, I asked Deena, "Where are you going?"

"To visit family in Indy." She said it in almost a snarl.

"How long will you be gone?"

She huffed. "I don't know."

CHAPTER TWELVE

TARA

Abby came over with Seedy around seven. We went into the living room where Seedling ran up to his basket of toys, grabbed his favorite squeaky chicken, and dropped it at his mother's feet. When Seedy went to pick it up, Seedling grabbed onto the long yellow feet and held on. A tug of war ensued.

I took her jacket and hung it up in the hall closet. "I've got news."

The pizza I'd ordered arrived and Aunt Abby and I sat down at the kitchen table to eat. We each took a slice and then she said, "You look like the cat who swallowed the canary. What's going on?"

"Deena's mom is alive."

My aunt lowered the slice. "She's is?"

"I went over to Deena's house this evening, and while I was there, her mother came into her room and told her to pack her bag. Deena said they were going to visit family in Indianapolis."

"To see her grandmother?"

"She didn't say. And she doesn't know how long she'll be gone."

Aunt Abby chewed a bite of pizza. "Did Deena seem concerned?"

"Not so much concerned as angry." I polished off my slice and took another. "I'm telling you, something is going on with Mr. Allen. You know what I think it is? I think he's on the run."

"From what?"

"From the police. I told you how he was out in his shed in the middle of the night right after the police had been there. And now suddenly they're taking a trip?"

"It's odd, Tara, but it's not illegal. Tracy is alive. Deena isn't in danger. What more do you want?"

"I want to know what Deena's dad was keeping in his shed. I want to know why they're taking a last-minute trip out of town."

"Keep a watch on their house. I bet they'll be back in time for school on Monday."

"What about the shed?" I asked.

Abby picked up another slice. "I think it's time you let this one go. Some mysteries just aren't meant to be solved."

ABBY

Sunday

Bloomers wasn't open to the public on Sundays, but early that morning, I'd checked the orders that had come in through our website and saw a number of them for Frank Vesco's visitation to be held that afternoon. So I called my team together and we met at Bloomers at ten o'clock.

The visitation was set for two o'clock, and by one-thirty, Lottie had delivered all thirteen arrangements, and Rosa and I were on our way home. When I got there, Marco was dressed and ready to go. I changed into something appropriate and we set off for Happy Dreams Funeral Home.

When we arrived, we were directed to Parlor A, where we found a line of people waiting to speak with Eileen, standing in front of a closed casket. After we'd signed our names in the guest book, Marco ran his finger down the list. "Here's Michael's name, but I don't see Eileen's."

"I don't think she would sign the guest book."

"Then we'll have to find another way to compare her signature." Marco took out his cell phone and snapped a photo of the names when I heard, "Marco, Abby," and turned to see Michael walking up to us.

With a quick glance in Marco's direction, I stepped in front of him and said, "Once again, our deepest condolences, Michael."

"It's so nice of you to come," he said with a smile.

Marco moved up beside me. "Quite a crowd."

Michael nodded. "He was a good man." He looked around at the crowd and lowered his voice, suddenly very serious. "That's why I decided to ask around, see if there was anyone with a motive to hurt Uncle Frank, and I think there's something you should know. Maybe we can step into the refreshment room and talk there."

Michael led the way out of Parlor A and up a hallway to a smaller room equipped with two easy chairs in one corner and a long table against a wall. On the table were a coffee maker, a hot water dispenser, cardboard take-out cups, plastic spoons, paper napkins, and a large plate with an assortment of cookies on it. Michael immediately took a cup and held it beneath the coffee dispenser, then added creamer. He turned to us as he blew on the coffee to cool it off. "Want anything?"

"No, thanks," I said, digging in my purse for the small notebook and pen.

"Not for me either, thanks," Marco said, then looked around. "Let's move into that corner." He indicated the farthest corner of the room.

After a few people had cleared the area, Michael opened up. "I was thinking about the life insurance policy you told me about, how coincidental the timing was, so I talked to Frank's secretary and we went over the policy, and the date it was issued . . ." He looked around before continuing. "You were right. The policy kicked in one year after the issue date, and as of today, it's been one year and two weeks. Now, that would make sense if Frank was depressed or desperate, if he wanted to end his life for the benefit of his family, but that wasn't the case. There is only one person who would benefit from Uncle Frank's death."

"His wife," I said.

Michael nodded, "And after a little investigation of my own, I found out that Eileen was having an affair and Frank knew about it."

I wrote down the information, completely confirming my intuition about Frank's wife. Never once had she moved from number one on my suspect list.

"Here's my theory," Michael continued. "Frank wasn't planning a fishing trip. His secretary did indeed set up the reservation, but did he go? I don't think so. I talked to John, and we both agreed that Frank must've been up to something."

"Like what?" Marco asked.

He shrugged. "Maybe he stayed behind to watch his wife. Maybe he found out what she was doing and confronted her. All I know is that Frank did not extend his fishing trip.

Whatever happened in the days leading up to his death is a mystery, but I would guarantee that Eileen was behind it."

I stopped writing. "Eileen is your aunt, right?"

"She's my aunt, yeah, and I love her to death, but I loved my uncle, too. He was like a father to me. And if I'm wrong, then I'll admit to it. That's why I'm telling you first. Prove me wrong. Come back and tell me that I'm wrong. Please." Michael started to tear up. He pulled a handkerchief from his pocket, wiped his eyes quickly, and inhaled, trying to shake it off.

"We'll do what we can," I said.

"I should probably get back," Michael said. He shook both of our hands and left the room.

Marco looked at me. "I think we're done here."

"What's your impression of Michael?" Marco asked me.

"I don't get the sense that he's involved. He's been very helpful, but as we've learned in the past, sometimes that helpful person is being that way for a reason."

"He said there was only one person who benefited from Frank's death, but that isn't true." Marco pulled out of the parking lot and headed toward town. "Michael also benefits by inheriting Frank's business."

"He could be throwing his aunt under the bus," I said. "But if he's the killer, he's done a great job convincing me otherwise."

"That's why I want to compare the handwriting. When I get back, I'm going to print out the photo I took of Michael's and Eileen's signatures. Hopefully, Reilly will be sending me a photo of the suicide note soon."

My cell phone rang, and Tara's name popped up on the screen. "Hey, kiddo, what's up?"

"Do you want to pick up some carry-out for dinner tonight?" Tara asked.

"Why don't you come over to my house? I was going to make chicken tacos. You can help me."

"Awesome. What time?"

"Dinner's at seven o'clock, so come over anytime."

"Sounds great."

As I slipped my cell phone back into my purse, Marco looked at me askance. "What?" I asked.

"Tara's coming over," he said.

"And?"

"And you'll end up talking all night about the dead body in the shed."

"No, we won't," I said. "Besides, why would that be a bad thing?"

"You're encouraging her."

"I am not."

"Anyway," Marco said irritably, "I was hoping we could do some reconnoitering this evening."

"Of whom?"

"Eileen Vesco. Visitation ends at six, so I thought we could do a little stakeout after dinner."

"Marco, it's the evening before the funeral. What are you hoping to discover?"

"I'm acting on a hunch, Abby. You have your inner radar. I have hunches."

"The problem is, I can't abandon Tara. Either she comes with us, or you have to go alone."

"She's not coming with." He stared straight ahead.

"Fine." I stared out my side window.

And that was how we left it.

✿❀✿

We ate dinner at seven then sat around the table talking about the dead body in the shed. I tried to sway the conversation every time Marco smirked at me, but Tara was relentless.

"Uncle Marco, you've been too quiet. What do you think about the Allens?"

"Who are the Allens?" Marco asked.

"The people who live behind me," she said. "The ones with the creepy shed where the dead body was hidden."

"I thought that case was solved," Marco said, glancing my way.

"We know the wife came home," I said, "but Tara still believes something sinister happened in that shed."

"It didn't happen in the shed," she corrected. "He only used the shed to hide the body. Then after the police came, he got scared and dragged the body out."

"And we know it was a dead body because?" Marco asked.

"What else could it have been?" she asked. "It was long and bulky and obviously heavy. And when I looked inside the shed, I could've sworn I saw bloodstains."

Marco scoffed.

"Come on, Uncle M," Tara said. "He dragged it in the middle of the night. Who does that? And then yesterday he rounded up the family for an unexpected trip out of town, and he wouldn't say how long they were going to be gone. I think he's on the run."

"Tara," Marco said. "I think you watch too many TV mystery shows."

My niece looked at me with a sour face. "He doesn't believe me."

"That's okay," I told her. "He doesn't believe me either."

Marco closed his eyes and pinched the bridge of his nose, slowly shaking his head.

"Let's watch a movie before we head back to your house," I said.

Tara hopped up from her chair and headed for the living room. "How about an Alfred Hitchcock movie? I know the perfect one."

Marco pointed at me. "Don't encourage her."

This time I was the one with the sour face.

✿❀✿

Marco left the house fifteen minutes before eight and didn't call me until almost midnight. I was reading in bed in Tara's guest room when my phone vibrated. "How did it go?"

"Let's just say I'm glad I went."

"What happened?"

"You know the office building we followed Eileen to yesterday? She went back today."

"Shouldn't offices be closed on Sundays?"

"She waited outside the main entrance until a man came to the door and let her in. She left an hour later, so I followed her back to her house where she parked her car in the garage. Here's where it gets really interesting. About ten minutes later, a car turned into her driveway, the garage door opened, and the car pulled into the garage next to her car."

"Did you see the driver's face?"

"No, but I know it was a man. When he got out of the car, Eileen came up to him and they kissed."

I sat up in bed. "Sounds like Eileen Vesco has a boyfriend."

"Sounds like Eileen Vesco has a motive for murder."

I swung my legs off the bed and sat up. "Then Michael was right about Eileen sneaking around."

"That's how it appears. I waited around until almost midnight to see if the man would leave, but the lights in the house turned off, so I assumed he was staying."

"Wow. She didn't even wait until after the funeral."

"I'm going to go back to Eileen's early tomorrow morning. I want to see where this man goes."

"Okay. Keep me posted."

CHAPTER THIRTEEN

ABBY

Monday

Breakfast at Bloomers was the rule for Mondays, so I started the day with a plate full of Rosa's delicious *Huevos Marisol* and a cup of Grace's pumpkin spice coffee. We discussed business matters after we'd eaten, then set off to our workstations in time to open the shop.

More orders had come in overnight for Frank's funeral, so we had to have them done and get them delivered by three o'clock. Marco and I had decided that we wouldn't attend the funeral, but Marco was going to continue his stake-out of Eileen Vesco.

Shortly after noon, as I was grabbing a quick bite of lunch, Tara called. "Aunt Abby, guess what? Deena didn't show up today! I told you something was fishy about that trip."

"Okay, I have some time right now. I'll call Deena's grandmother and see what she knows."

"Text me when you find out. I'll be at lunch for another thirty minutes."

I hung up and searched through my phone for Alice Bailey's number. I called it but it went to voice mail, so I left a message asking her to call me. I texted Tara: *No luck. I'll keep you posted.* Then I went back to the workroom to finish the orders.

At three o'clock Lottie left to make deliveries, so I went up to the showroom to wait on customers. I had just rung up a bouquet of orange and yellow mums for a pair of women when Jillian popped in.

"Thank you for coming in," I said to the women, then turned to see Jillian taking off a dark red long coat.

"Isn't that a new coat?" I asked.

She turned toward me wearing a matching deep red dress.

"And isn't that a new dress?" I asked, staring at her open-mouthed. "Jillian!"

"Yes, it's a new coat and, yes, it's a new dress. Yes, yes, yes! I couldn't stand it any longer, okay? I need clothes!" She put her hands over her face and shook her head. "I'm pathetic, aren't I?"

I went over and put my arm around her back. "Jillian, it's okay. You're not pathetic. You like clothes. There's no harm in that. Think of it this way. When you buy new things, your very nice older things can go to a new home."

She put down her hands and turned to me, throwing her arms around me to give me a big hug. Then she held me at arm's length. "Yes! That's exactly what I'll do. Every time I buy something new, I'll donate something." She crushed me against her again and then turned away. "I feel as though a weight has lifted off my shoulders. Thank you."

I breathed in deeply and held her at arm's length. "Is that new perfume?"

She held up her nose. "I said thank you for the wonderful advice, Abs. Let's leave it at that."

"You're welcome. Do you want to have a cup of tea with me?"

She slipped on her new coat. "No time. There's a sale going on at Windows on the Square." She parted the curtain to leave. "Tell Grace I'll have some donations for her tomorrow."

At three-thirty, Tara came hurrying in through the purple curtain, tossing her backpack on my desk chair and hopping up onto a stool. "Any word from the grandma?"

"No, nothing."

"Aunt Abby, Deena missed a geometry test today and she can't afford that. I know she wouldn't have done that willingly. I'm telling you; Mr. Allen is on the run."

"It's Doctor Allen."

"Oh, right." She thought for a moment. "Wouldn't a doctor have to see patients? How can he just up and leave his job?"

"He's a psychologist, but yes, you'd think so." I opened my laptop and did a search for Dr. Paul Allen. I came up with a listing for him under *New Chapel Marriage Counselors.*

I dialed the number while Tara stared at me in anticipation. "What are you going to say?"

"I'm going to ask when Dr. Allen will be back. As you said, a doctor needs to see patients."

The phone rang twice before a secretary picked up. "Dr. Allen's office."

"Hi, I'd like to make an appointment with Dr. Allen as soon as possible."

Tara leaned in closer to listen. I could tell she was loving every minute of this investigation. She reminded me so much of myself, but with twice the determination I'd had at her age. I put the phone on speaker so she could hear.

"There's an opening next Friday at noon. Are you a current patient?"

"Is there anything sooner? It's - an emergency."

"I'm sorry to hear that. I can certainly try to squeeze you in sometime today or tomorrow. Can I get your name?"

Tara looked confused and mouthed the same words I was thinking. *Today or tomorrow?*

"Dr. Allen is in the office today?"

"Yes. May I please have your name?"

"On second thought," I said, "I'll have to call you back."

"Aunt Abby, what in the world is going on?" Tara asked as I ended the call. "He takes his family out of town but then goes to work every day? That doesn't make sense unless he's up to something."

I set the phone down and thought for a moment. "He must have taken his family to see their grandmother and returned home for work."

Tara snapped her fingers. "Or maybe he's just using work as an excuse to come home and clean out the shed. Do you see why we need to get a look inside? He hasn't been back home yet, but I'll be he will soon, and then he'll remove all the evidence."

"What we should do is call the police and have them look. But before they'll do that, we'll have to have solid evidence that Paul Allen committed a crime."

"Can't we just ask the police to check the shed for that evidence?"

"Not without good reason."

"Then what can we do?"

I looked back over the information for Dr. Allen, thinking. I noticed the office address looked familiar, so I did a map search and gasped. "Oh, my God."

"What is it?" Tara asked, leaning over my arm.

"This is the building."

"What building?"

"We followed a woman named Eileen Vesco to a building the other night, and this is it."

"What does that mean?"

I closed the laptop. "Eileen is a suspect that Marco and I have been investigating. She went to see Dr. Allen, a marriage counselor, after her husband had been dead for over a week."

"I'm still not following."

I turned to Tara. "The body in the shed was Eileen's husband."

The color in Tara's face went pale and she turned to face away from me.

"What's wrong?" I asked.

She turned halfway but didn't look at me. "I don't know. It just didn't seem real until now."

I waited a few moments before giving my niece a hug, understanding too well the gravity of our situation. "It's not easy to deal with. I know. I'm sorry."

After a few moments, Tara collected herself and looked at me. "He killed someone, Aunt Abby," she said as she wiped her eyes. "And he needs to pay."

I looked at my watch. "I have an idea, but it's something I'm going to have to do, Tara, without Uncle Marco's help."

"And that is?"

"Go see a marriage counselor."

Because we'd finished up all of our orders for the day, I was able to leave Bloomers at five-thirty to put my plan into action. It was such a beautiful autumn day that I decided to walk the six blocks to the low, flat brick building that housed Dr. Allen's office. I took the time to clear my head and put all of the clues into place.

Frank Vesco was reported missing around the same time that Tara saw Dr. Allen dragging a body into his tool shed. Eileen Vesco claimed that she had received text messages from Frank, knowing the body was soon to be disposed of. She must have used Frank's phone to send the messages to herself and the other members of her family. Then she could've given the phone to Dr. Allen to place near Frank's body in the woods. She either wrote the suicide note herself or had her lover forge the note for her. Franks' body was then found one day after the police showed up at Dr. Allen's house. He must've been so scared that he dragged away Frank's body that same night.

All of the pieces fit. All of the clues pointed in one direction. Eileen Vesco and Dr. Paul Allen planned the murder of Frank Vesco. My first instinct was to call Marco, to let him know that we were both on the right track this whole time, but I wanted to be absolutely sure that Dr. Allen was involved. I needed to speak to him, to look him in the eyes and gauge his reaction when I brought up the subject.

And if luck was on my side, I might even get enough evidence to share with the police. I lifted my phone from my pocket and opened the voice recorder as I rounded the corner of his building. Inside the main entrance, I found a directory listing the suite numbers of the various businesses. Dr. Allen's suite was number four.

I hadn't planned exactly what to say to him. First, I wanted to see whether Allen was still at work. Then it depended on whether I could get him to see me. If I could, I'd have to come up with some sort of marital problem to discuss with him, then subtly slip in my questions.

I walked into suite four and stopped in surprise. There stood Marco, talking to the receptionist. He mirrored my stunned look that said, *What are you doing here?*

The receptionist glanced from him to me.

"Here you are, Marco," I said, forcing cheerfulness in my tone. "I wondered whether you got my message."

"Yes," he said, bouncing back from his surprise. "Thanks for letting me know you'd be here." He'd tried to put a good twist on it, but I knew he was being facetious.

I walked up to the receptionist and smiled. "I'm sure my husband already asked, but is Dr. Allen in?"

"Yes, but I'm afraid he's booked for the day. I can fit you in this Friday however."

"Apparently," Marco said to me, "Dr. Allen took a few days off and is trying to make up for it by working late every evening."

"Ah," I said. "But nothing's available until the end of the week?"

She scanned her appointment book. "I'm afraid not."

I looked at Marco. He folded his arms and stared down at me as if to challenge my skills. I took his stance to imply that if he couldn't do it, neither could I. I turned back to the receptionist. "We spoke earlier on the phone and you said you might be able to squeeze me in sometime today."

"That's right," she said. "But I'm afraid Dr. Allen is almost done for the day. "Would you like to schedule something for tomorrow?" She smiled at me, waiting.

I glanced at Marco, hoping that he had something up his sleeve, but Marco just shrugged. Not knowing what else to do I said, "Sure."

The phone rang and the receptionist answered, giving Marco and I a chance to talk. I stepped out of earshot and Marco joined me.

"What are you doing here?" he asked.

"Dr. Allen and Eileen Vesco are having an affair," I whispered.

"Yes, Sunshine. I've gathered that. It's why I'm here."

"Marco, Dr. Allen is Tara's neighbor. He dragged the body into the shed. The body of Frank Vesco."

A door across the room opened and a large man with brown hair stuck his head out. "Sarah, you can send in my next appointment."

"I'm sorry, but your five-thirty just called. They won't be able to make it." She looked over at us and brightened. "But this couple would like to see you."

"Good." He waved us in. "I can see you now."

CHAPTER FOURTEEN

ABBY

"Tell me a little about yourself, Abby."

I appraised the man sitting across from us in an overstuffed armchair. He was a big man with thinning brown hair, an oval face, dark eyes, and a long chin. He had a notepad in his lap and a pen in his left hand. A leftie.

"I'm a florist. I own a flower shop called Bloomers on the town square right here in New Chapel. You may have heard of it. I also have a cute little, three-legged rescue dog and a beautiful Russian Blue cat."

He wrote it down. "Interesting that you felt it important to mention that your dog has three legs."

I stared at him.

He turned to my husband, sitting beside me on a beige tweed sofa. "And Marco, tell me about you."

"I own Down the Hatch Bar and Grill also on the town square. I'm a former Army Ranger."

Dr. Allen gave a little smile and wrote it down. "Being a former Army Ranger is important to you, isn't it?"

Marco glanced at me as if to say, *Is this guy for real?*

"Just part of my bio."

"I see. Abby, what do you see as the strengths in your relationship with Marco?"

I looked at my sexy hubby, with his dark hair that drooped casually onto his forehead and curled at the back of his neck, his soulful brown eyes, his square jaw, his expressive mouth, his broad shoulders . . .

I shook myself out of my reverie and focused. "Well, we love each other. That's a strength. We trust each other. We're there for each other. We have many of the same likes . . ." I paused, wanting to say more nice things, but this was supposed to be a marriage counseling session. What could I possibly say was wrong with our relationship?

"Okay," Dr. Allen said. "And you, Marco?"

Marco gazed into my eyes, a smile curving his mouth at the corners. "Ditto."

"Could you express your feelings?"

"I feel the same way Abby does."

That was my husband, a man of few words. A man of action, integrity. A man I loved with all my heart.

Dr. Allen looked from me to Marco. "So what brings you two here today?"

And now the acting began.

I started. "We're having problems communicating. I feel like I'm not heard when I speak to him."

"Marco, is that a fair statement?"

Marco rubbed his chin. "I don't know about fair. Maybe I've been a little short lately."

"And why are you being short with your wife?"

Marco glanced at me again. "I think sometimes she may be a little too impulsive. It's hard to communicate that without hurting her feelings."

I was starting to wonder if this was really an act. "I'm impulsive?"

Marco squeezed my hand, which was our signal to go along with it. "I'm sorry, babe. Adorably impulsive. But sometimes I worry about you."

I squeezed back, harder than he had. "What do you worry about, sweetheart?"

"I worry that you'll get yourself in a situation and I won't be able to help you."

"I don't always need your help," I said.

Marco tried to hide his smile. "Disregard my comment," he said and squeezed my hand again. "Let's move on to more important topics."

I pulled my hand away. "Says someone who's a *little* too controlling."

Marco looked at me in surprise. "Too controlling?"

I gave him a tight smile. "As I said, a little."

"In what way?" the counselor asked.

I glanced at Dr. Allen. He was eating this up. Our ruse was working. Maybe a little *too* well.

They were both watching me now, waiting for my answer. "You like to schedule every minute of the day. Sometimes I just like to kick back and relax."

"You know I have to do that because –" Marco caught himself. "You're right. I do schedule things. I'll have to work on that."

"Let's go over some tools for you to use, Marco. We can start with –" The counselor glanced at the clock on the wall, stopping mid-sentence. He seemed to shift uncomfortably in his chair before standing and walking to his desk. "We'll have to end it there for today." He sat down and shuffled some papers on his desk until he found a folder. "I have a worksheet in here and some questionnaires I would like both of you to fill out, just some tools to help with communication."

I took out my notebook and pen and prepared to write. "I noticed on the website that your office closes at six o'clock. Is that correct?"

"That's right."

"But you have a patient scheduled after six?" I asked.

As if I'd just threatened him in some way, he looked down at me with a cold glare. "My hours vary depending on the patient."

Marco chimed in. "Before we leave, I would like to let you know that a client of yours recommended you. She spoke very highly of you as well." He looked at me as if to ask permission to proceed.

I smiled at him and nodded.

"Her name is Eileen Vesco."

At the name, Dr. Allen sat upright in his chair. He didn't say a word as his eyes darted between us. Finally, he responded, "I don't have a patient by that name."

Marco retrieved his phone from his pocket and pulled up the photos he'd taken. He scrolled through and turned the phone to Dr. Allen. "Does this look familiar to you? This was taken outside of your office on Saturday night, and this was taken at Eileen's house last night."

Dr. Allen studied the photos. His manner was even and professional, but his breathing was unsteady, and his words came out forced. "I don't know who that is. I think you should leave now."

"We'll leave, Dr. Allen," I said. "But when we do, we're going straight to the police station. I think they'll be very interested to see these pictures."

"Those pictures prove nothing," Allen said, standing. "You need to leave."

Marco raised to his feet. "What were you dragging into the shed last Sunday night?"

I stood up next to him as Allen rounded his desk and came forward, brushing past Marco, opening the door, and pointing through the exit forcefully. "Leave!"

We did as he demanded, but I continued, "If you have information, Dr. Allen, I suggest you pay a visit to the police before they come looking for you."

We left the building and walked to Marco's Prius parked along the curb. I turned off the voice recorder and saved the file, even though we didn't get a confession, but Tara would be happy to hear that we finally confronted him.

"What do you think he's going to do?" I asked.

"I have no idea. That was the most impromptu interview we've ever done. Good job, by the way. You were very clever in there."

"You did pretty well yourself," I said. "I didn't expect you to bring up the shed."

He held my shoulders. "Why?"

"I didn't think you were really listening. You just dismissed everything when I would try to talk to you."

He laughed. "That's what I do. I dismiss all the unbelievable scenarios, like Tara witnessing her neighbor dragging the dead body of the missing man that we just happened to be investigating. How unbelievable does that sound?"

"But it happened."

He leaned down to kiss me. "Where's your car?"

"I walked."

Marco opened his passenger door for me. I watched him walk in front of the car, my handsome hubby, but I couldn't shake the feeling that our marriage counseling session had been more than just a ruse. Instead of pressing the subject when he joined me, I asked, "What's our next move?"

"I'll call Reilly and let him know what we've found, but I'm afraid Dr. Allen was right. The pictures are just circumstantial evidence. I didn't get a clear shot of him or his car in any of the photos, so I'll have to continue my stakeout. Hopefully, the detectives will pick up the investigation from there."

"And I'll be at Tara's until Saturday, so we can keep our eye on the house. If there is evidence in the shed, he might want to clean it out."

Marco reached over to hold my hand. He squeezed it, just like he had in the counselor's office. "If you see any suspicious activity, call the police immediately. Do not go over there."

"Are you worried my impulsivity will get me into trouble?"

He glanced at me and smirked. "It always does."

I secured the seatbelt as Marco put the car in reverse. "You really worry about me?"

Marco looked at me. "A little."

"In what way?"

He rubbed his hands over the steering wheel. "You have a slight tendency to put yourself in harm's way."

"A *slight* tendency. Like being a *little* impulsive."

"I had to come up with something, Sunshine."

"And that was the only thing you could think of?"

"I wanted it to be realistic."

I was silent.

Marco glanced at me. "Do you think I'm too controlling?"

"Well, you do like to take charge."

"And schedule down to the minute?"

"It was the only thing I could come up with quickly."

"You realize that in order to run the bar and the PI business, maintain the lawn at the house, and have enough time left over to spend with you and the pets, I have to have a schedule."

"Marco, I didn't say having a schedule was a bad thing. Actually, it's – to coin a phrase, adorable." Then I added facetiously, "Just like my impulsiveness."

Marco quickly changed the subject.

✿❀✿

Tara was practically jumping as she listened to the audio of our interview with Dr. Allen. I'd picked up some take-out for dinner and we sat at the table listening to the recording, but my mind was still on the car ride home. As always, Marco had scheduled his night right down to the minute, and I had to admit that he'd had a point about scheduling. We were both busy and there was no way we'd get anything done if not for careful planning, but I didn't realize that I'd had an issue with it until it came out of my mouth.

After walking Seedy and grabbing a bite to eat, Marco was going to stake out Eileen's house and try to get more evidence of collusion between the two. I was to watch the neighbor's house to see if Dr. Allen made any more trips to the shed. Luckily, communication was not a problem with us, even though it seemed like my impulsivity may have been. I'd have to work on that, too.

"I can't believe you just walked in and accused him of murder. Go Auntie A! I wish I could've seen the look on his stupid face. I knew I was right. I knew it!"

"You did good, Tara. Now we wait and see if he comes home."

"Are you kidding? We can't wait. We need evidence. What if he comes home late at night and we're asleep? There are bloodstains in that shed, Aunt Abby."

"We're not breaking into private property. If we see Dr. Allen come home, we're calling the police and that's that."

"We don't have to break in," Tara said, but then stopped herself. She looked down at her food and toyed with it.

"What?" I asked.

"Nothing."

"Then it's settled."

TARA

Abby is wrong, I texted David. *There's evidence of a crime inside that shed and we need to find it.*

Wish I could help, he texted back. *I'm about to pass out. You know we have school tomorrow?*

I put my phone down and picked up the binoculars, training them on the house across the yard. It was nearly midnight and there'd been no sign of activity at the Allen house all evening. It would be a snap to dash across the yard and open up the shed. After all, I had the key.

Marco had called Abby before bed to let her know that Dr. Allen had once again visited Eileen Vesco. He said the lights were off and the car was parked in the garage, so Marco decided to end the stakeout for the night. Dr. Allen was definitely not coming back to his house. I could be back in ten minutes and no one would ever know. But Abby was insistent that we wait for the police to handle it.

I set the binoculars down. *Wait for what?*

I put on my jacket, felt for the key in the pocket, and quietly slipped out into the hallway. The door to the guest room was closed. Aunt Abby was asleep. She might be upset that I disobeyed her, but she'd get over it once she saw the photos and we put Dr. Allen in prison. I was sure of it.

Moving stealthily, I made my way downstairs to the back door where I opened it quietly and stepped outside. It was nearly pitch black, only a little light coming from the moon in the cloudy sky. I sidestepped the motion-detecting floodlights, dashed across the yard, pausing by the woodpile alongside the shed to scan the back of the Allen house, then snuck around to the front and slipped the key from my pocket.

My hands were shaking as I opened the lock. I pulled back the latch and swung the shed door open, causing it to creak loudly. I pulled my cell phone from my pocket and switched on the flashlight. The inside of the shed lit up. I shone the light around the interior. Wooden shelves lined two of the walls, filled with jars of nails and screws, a red tool chest, a staple gun, cans of insect spray, boxes of grass seed, and fertilizer.

On the floor backed against the wall was a riding lawn mower with a bag attached to one side. In the corner stood a rake, a snow shovel, and a broom.

An old calendar was nailed to the wall near the small window. I started toward it only to have my foot slip. I glanced down to see what had caused it and found a thick screw under my shoe. And under the screw – a dark brownish-red stain.

I glanced around my feet and saw that the stain was spread out over an area of about two feet wide by two feet deep, an irregular stain that looked like something red had spilled. I stepped back in surprise as the truth hit me. I was standing in the middle of what had been a puddle of blood.

I pulled out my phone and snapped as many pictures as I could. Then I texted my aunt the photos. This was too important to wait. *I was right!* I texted. *Blood in the shed!*

Suddenly I heard the sound of voices coming my way. I ran to the lawnmower and squeezed behind it, ducking down behind the clippings bag.

"Someone's been here," I heard Dr. Allen say. "Check the shed."

"Didn't you lock it up?"

"Of course, I did, but someone stole the spare key and I think I know who it was."

My hands were shaking as the beam of light flashed above my head and around the sides of the lawnmower. I looked down at the phone in my hands, not even thinking about how loud my phone would be if Abby responded. I tried to steady my breathing, wondering if I could just run as fast as I could, knocking over anyone who stood in my way.

But my legs wouldn't move. They felt weak and unsteady as I stayed knelt behind the mower. My fingers trembled as I tried to type a message to my aunt.

"We'll have to work fast. I hope the bleach works. The detergent didn't touch it."

My heart raced as I listened to Dr. Allen and a woman talking. I heard the sound of something rough rubbing against the floor, then a muttered curse. I heard Dr. Allen get to his feet.

"It's not working. The blood has soaked in and dried."

"What now?" the woman asked.

"We burn the shed."

CHAPTER FIFTEEN

ABBY

I was almost asleep when my phone dinged. I reached for the phone on the nightstand and read the text message: *I was right! Blood in the shed!*

I sat up and threw back the covers. Tara was in the Allen's shed.

I dressed quickly and hurried downstairs, slipping on my warm jacket and shoes and dashing to the back door. I stepped outside and was immediately bathed in bright white light. I stopped as everything around me lit up and shielded my eyes.

Once off the back deck, the darkness seemed overwhelming, my eyes now spotted with white circles. I had to readjust before starting across the yard. I got as far as the big oak tree in Tara's yard and saw a light flicker between the wooden slats of the shed. What was Tara doing?

I ran up to a large pile of wood and stopped at the sound of voices, two of them, a man's and a woman's, coming from inside the shed.

Where was Tara?

I crouched down behind the woodpile and called Marco. "Pick up, pick up, pick up," I whispered. And then his voice came on the line.

"Abby?"

"Marco, I need you to call the police. I'm in the yard behind Tara's house and I can hear Dr. Allen and Eileen Vesco talking. I don't know where Tara is."

"Okay, I'll call the police. Stay safe. I'm on my way."

I slipped my phone back into my jacket, crept around the woodpile up to the side of the shed near the open door, and listened.

I heard Allen swear. "I left the gas can in the trunk of my car."

"Paul, we can't burn down the shed with a girl inside. Are you crazy?"

Dear God, they'd found Tara.

"We have no choice now. The fire will burn away the evidence. It'll just look like a neighborhood kid lit a fire and got trapped."

"Paul, this is terrible. I want nothing to do with this."

"You should've thought about that before you killed your husband. Now stay here and watch her until I get back with the gasoline."

My heart was pounding as I watched Allen set off toward the house. I waited until he'd gone around the side, no doubt heading for the garage in front, then I picked up a thick log from the woodpile, snuck up to the open door, and swung it with all my might into the back of Eileen Vesco's legs. She buckled and reeled backward through the door and onto the ground just outside.

Tara jumped out from behind the mower and I took her hand, pulling her toward me.

"Behind you!" Tara cried.

I turned to see Allen running toward the shed. Before he could reach us, Eileen slammed the door shut, leaving us in pitch blackness. I reached out for Tara, pulling her close. "Are you alright?"

"I'm so sorry," she said, her voice shaky. "I tried to run but Mr. Allen stopped me. He threatened me with a knife and took my phone."

I reached for mine, shining the light around the shed, looking for anything that could protect us. I could see a gas can, bug spray, pesticides, and other flammable objects. Then I saw the gardening tools and picked up a trowel.

"Hurry," I heard Eileen shout.

Tara grabbed me by the arm. I heard the click of the padlock and then the sound of liquid being splashed against the outside wall. I dropped the trowel. They were going to burn us alive.

"You won't get away with this!" I cried. I banged my shoulder against the door, but it held firm. I could smell the gasoline as it soaked into the walls. It was only a matter of seconds before the shed was set on fire.

Tara squeezed my hand. "I'm so sorry, Aunt Abby. What are we going to do?"

"The police are on the way," I told her, then called Marco, leaving the flashlight on, scanning the room for a way out. "How close are you?"

"I'm almost there. I didn't know the address, so I gave the police Tara's address."

"It's the house directly behind Tara's. Marco, Allen is about to start the shed on fire. We're trapped inside."

Tara clutched my hand hard enough to make me wince. "I'm scared."

"Abby, I'll be there in a minute."

I glanced down to see a curl of gray smoke snaking up from the baseboard on the side wall. "We don't have a minute."

"Is there anything you can use to cover your face?"

I shined the light around and saw a red bandana lying on a shelf. I grabbed it and handed it to Tara. "Cover your mouth and nose."

"What about you?" she cried.

I couldn't think about myself. All I could think about was Marco at the counselor's office, telling him that he was too controlling, justifying my impulsivity, and dismissing his concerns about my safety.

"Marco, I want to apologize for what I said earlier. I'm sorry for being so impulsive. I should've listened to you."

"Sweetheart, listen to me now. Is there a window you can climb through?"

I hurried to the window. The glass had been broken, leaving splintered pieces sticking out. Behind the glass were thick boards nailed around the frame. "It's boarded up."

An orange glow burned brightly through the window and I could hear flames licking the sides of the shed. The smoke billowed in through the slats, causing my lungs to burn. I started to tear up. "Marco, I love you. I'm so sorry."

Tara wrapped her arms around me and sobbed. I held her tight, thinking of all the things I wished I could tell Marco. I thought of my mom and dad, how I wished I could tell them how much I loved them, too. I thought of Seedy and Smoke, my sweet pets.

The heat came from all sides. I pulled the flammable cans from the shelves on the wall and directed Tara to do the same. Once the walls were clear we tried to push the mower away, but it was too heavy to move.

A loud bang made us both jump. At first, I thought something had exploded and I pulled Tara close to me, but then I heard someone calling her name.

"It's David." Tara cried. "David, we're trapped inside!"

"Hold on!" he shouted.

The fire began to burn through the back wall. In moments, it would reach the riding mower and the bag hanging on the side. When it hit the engine, I knew there would be a gas explosion.

Suddenly I heard a loud hiss coming from the shed door. Dark smoke crept beneath the door and I could hear water being sprayed against it.

"Tara," David called. "Cover your face."

"Get the back wall!" I shouted as the flames spread up the wall behind the mower.

I pulled Tara to the wood floor, making sure her face was covered. Black smoke filled the space between us and all I could do was hold her and try not to breathe too deeply as the hissing continued around the perimeter of the shed.

Suddenly, something heavy hit the door. I could hear someone shout, "Stay back," and then several more loud cracks at the door before it burst open. I pulled Tara to her feet and helped her out and then I was in Marco's arms, being carried away from the shed. My lungs were burning, and tears filled my eyes, but I could see him, my husband, shouting instructions to the police as they rounded the sides of the house.

✿❀✿

As firemen pulled a large hose across the yard, Marco sat with me on the ground a safe distance away and hugged me tightly. Not far away, David sat with Tara, rocking her as she wept. An ambulance arrived next, along with Sgt. Reilly, who rushed to meet us, kneeling next to me, asking Marco questions.

I sat there in stunned silence as the firemen worked, but then a thought struck me. It wasn't over yet.

"You have to find Dr. Allen!" Tara cried. She crouched down beside me and faced Reilly. "He tried to kill us."

"And Eileen Vesco," I told Reilly. "She killed her husband and Dr. Allen helped her dispose of the body."

"You have to find them, Sergeant Reilly!" Tara cried.

Reilly rose and moved a short distance away, putting out a call from his shoulder radio.

With the firemen that evening had come the neighbors wanting to know what had happened. The police had held them back, telling them nothing. And we were too emotionally spent to even think about answering their questions. The only ones we had talked to were David's parents, who made it through the line of policemen to hug their son and listen to how he had rescued us. When he finished, his mother had tears in her eyes and his father hugged him fiercely.

Marco helped me up. "Tara, introduce me to this young man."

She turned to the boy standing beside her. "This is David. David, this is my Aunt Abby and Uncle Marco."

Marco shook his hand firmly. "You're a very brave man."

"Thank you," David said.

"How can I ever thank *you*?" Tara asked, looking up into his eyes.

"You don't need to thank me." He slipped off his high school jacket and wrapped Tara in it. "You're going to freeze."

She pulled her arms through the jacket and hugged him. He hugged her back.

TARA

I stayed home from school the next day, still in somewhat of a state of shock. It all felt surreal, the blood on the shed floor, hiding from the killers, Dr. Allen threatening me with a knife, Abby coming to find me, the smell of gas, the smoke burning my lungs. The scene played on repeat in my mind. I could hardly sleep the night before, and when I did, I dreamt of horrible things.

But the thrill lingered on.

The thrill of the chase, finding the clues, proving to everyone, including myself, that I was right, that feeling wouldn't leave me alone, and I wanted more.

Aunt Abby went into work late that morning, checking up on me before she left. I took my time getting up, checking my phone for a text from David, but saw that I had a text from Deena instead.

Deena: *I guess you know about my dad.*

Tara: *Yeah. I'm sorry.*

Deena: *I saw your article in the school newspaper online.*

Oh, no. I'd been so wrapped up in my own mystery that I didn't even think about how it would affect Deena. I typed a message, then erased it. What was I going to say?

Deena: *It's okay. I lied to you, too.*

Tara: *You did?*

Deena: *My mom wasn't in Colorado. She was at a church thing. I didn't tell you because I was embarrassed.*

Tara: *Why would you be embarrassed?*

Deena: *She went because she found out my dad was having an affair. She told me about it, and I didn't know what to say. My life is a mess right now.*

Tara: *It'll be okay.*

Deena: *New school +Dad in jail + No friends = Not okay.*

Tara: *You are so bad at math!*

Deena: *???*

Tara: *I'm your friend! And I'm not going anywhere. Call me tonight so we can talk. I have so much to tell you.*

I watched my phone, waiting for her response. Finally, I saw that she was typing.

Deena: *Thank you. That sounds awesome.*

Tara: *You are awesome. Tell Joy I said hi.*

Deena: *There is one good thing about living with my grandma, though.*

Tara: *What's that?*

Deena: *She makes the best brownies!*

I ended the conversation with a big smile on my face. I had started my investigation hoping to find a killer, but in the process, I ended up finding a very good friend.

I put down my phone and realized that I was going to have to call my parents eventually. I closed my eyes, trying to will myself back to sleep, but then Seedy and Seedling trampled through my room, giving chase under my bed. Seedling ended up perched on top of my stomach looking down at his mom, his tail wagging vigorously in front of my face.

"Okay, okay. I'm up."

Marco was in the kitchen reading the newspaper. He looked up at me and set the paper down as I joined him.

"There's toast and jam on the kitchen table. I can make eggs if you want."

"Toast is fine."

I sat down at the kitchen table. I could tell Marco was watching me, probably still thinking about last night. After we'd finished up with the police and the medics, we'd come back to the house. Too keyed up to sleep, Abby and I had gone over every detail of our investigation, every harrowing minute of the shed burning around us, and I was surprised that Marco had been so accepting and loving. He hadn't lectured, he hadn't been angry or condescending, only thankful that we'd made it out unscathed.

But now I had a feeling his mood had changed.

"Have you called your parents yet?" he asked.

"Not yet."

He joined me at the kitchen table as I set my toast down. "I'll call them after breakfast."

"And what will you tell them?"

"The truth."

"Okay," Marco said, "And what's the truth?"

I huffed. "They're not going to be happy with me. They're not understanding like you and Abby."

Marco smiled. I noticed he hadn't shaved. I wasn't used to seeing him with scruff. "I'm not as understanding as you might think. Abby and I stayed up pretty late last night talking about you."

"What about me?"

"You could've been seriously injured last night. And Abby, too."

"But we didn't, and we caught a killer. Two killers, actually."

"Tara, you didn't catch anyone. They caught you, and if David or I hadn't been there, I would be having this conversation with your grieving parents."

Suddenly I wasn't hungry. I pushed the plate away and sat in silence, thinking about what Marco had said. He got up from the table and left the room, coming back with my binoculars in his hand. "Where did you find those?"

"Abby found them in your suitcase."

"She went snooping in my room?"

"There's nothing wrong with snooping, isn't that what you told Abby? As long as the ends justify the means.

"Okay, I get it. I won't go snooping anymore."

"And you will tell your parents the whole truth. They won't be pleased with any of us, but you have to tell them before they hear from someone else. And absolutely no more snooping. Got it?"

I sighed. "Got it."

He smiled again. "You are just like your aunt."

"What? Don't you believe me?"

"I believe you, but just in case," he walked away, still holding the binoculars, "these stay with me."

ABBY

"Sweetie, you're lucky you're alive," Lottie said.

I was sitting at a wrought iron table in the coffee and tea parlor regaling Grace, Lottie, and Rosa with my story. When I finished, they all shook their heads in wonder.

"Will the story make the newspaper, do you think?" Grace asked, "because you might want to give your mum and dad a heads up."

"Good thinking, Grace."

Rosa crossed herself, muttering something in Spanish, and got up from the table, "No need to call them. Your mother is on her way." She pointed to a cardboard box full of candles by the cash register.

"Rosa, why aren't my mom's candles in the basement?"

"She told me to gather them for her." She raised her shoulders. "I did not ask."

My cell phone rang so I excused myself to answer it.

"Hello, Abby?" a woman said, "This is Alice Bailey. I'm sorry it took so long for me to return your call, but as you may know, things have been quite hectic here. I want you to know how thankful we are for your help. I'm sure once things calm down, Tracy will give you a call herself."

"Is Tracy there with you?" I asked.

"Yes, she and Deena and Joy are all here. They're a bit shaken up, but everyone is fine."

"I'm glad to hear that. My niece Tara was worried about Deena."

"No need to worry. My daughter and granddaughters are going to be living with me for a while. Deena will be attending school down here. I'll tell her to give Tara a call."

"I see. Any word on Dr. Allen?"

"No word yet, but I'm sure that monster will be caught very soon."

"I hope so. Take care, Mrs. Bailey."

Just before the store opened, my mom tapped on the big bay window and Rosa let her in. She was dressed as always in her school outfit, and as she came close to hug me, I could see her bright-red bloodshot eyes. "Hi, mom. What's wrong with your eyes?"

"Oh, it's just allergies," she said, blinking rapidly. "Nothing to worry about." She kept her arms wrapped around me as she continued. "You have to stop putting yourself in danger. I don't know what I would do if I lost my only daughter."

"How do you know already?"

"Reilly called your father this morning."

"I'm sorry, Mom. I'm starting to realize how impulsive I can be. I'm working on it."

She let go and looked around at Rosa, Grace, and Lottie with a smile. "Twenty-four murder investigations and now she's starting to realize." She rubbed her eyes. At first, I thought she'd started to cry, but then I understood what had happened. I followed my mom into the flower shop as she searched for her candles, her clothing smelling suspiciously of Mexican spice.

"Ah, Rosa, you have them all packed up for me. Thank you."

"What's going on with your dinner candles, Mom?"

"Oh, honey. After that horrible ordeal you just went through, I don't think it would be right to sell these anymore. I'll just take them away and dispose of them."

"It doesn't have anything to do with the spices you used in the candles?" I asked.

"Of course not. Besides, I've moved on to a new hobby. I can't wait to show you what I've been working on."

"Mom, did you light a candle last night?"

"Not another word, Abigail."

Marco, Tara, and I had just finished our dinner when the doorbell rang. Sergeant Sean Reilly came in with the news that

Dr. Paul Allen and Eileen Vesco had been caught at the Canadian border, passports in hand. They had already been brought back and questioned, and Dr. Allen had "flipped" on Eileen.

"He told us everything," Reilly said. "Frank Vesco came home early from his fishing trip and found his wife with Dr. Allen. There was a struggle, but Allen got the upper hand. After Frank was bound and moved to the basement, Eileen finished the job."

"He was killed at his own house," Marco said. "Why then would Dr. Allen drag the body into his own shed across town?"

Reilly sat back in the recliner across from Marco and I. Tara sat on the floor in front of us, hanging on Reilly's every word. He looked at Marco. "He didn't move the body until Sylvie Freeman came snooping around. Sylvie has a key to the house, so Eileen didn't feel comfortable keeping the body there."

"Why didn't they dispose of the body sooner?" I asked.

"They had to plan out the suicide," Reilly answered. "That takes time."

Marco interrupted. "I think they were already planning it. The timing of his death, the insurance policy, the passports, it seems too coincidental. My theory is that Frank knew about his wife cheating. He knew about the insurance policy and possibly even the plot against him. He set up this fishing trip as a decoy and stayed behind to catch them in the act."

"It's possible," Reilly commented. "They might've had to put their plan into action prematurely, which caused them to make mistakes. Eileen thought she could stall by sending text messages from Frank's phone. The investigation would've turned that up right away. Also, Frank was right-handed, but the handwriting analysis shows the note was written by a leftie."

"A leftie," I repeated. "I noticed Dr. Allen was left-handed at our counseling session."

At that, Reilly sat back in shock. "Counseling session?"

"Fake counseling, of course," I said. "But we don't have to get into that now."

"Well," Reilly continued. "Add one more nail to Allen's coffin. The handwriting would've been a dead giveaway if the detectives would've had time to work." He looked down at Tara.

"What about the blood in the shed?" she asked. "Is that still evidence or did it get burned away?"

"They had the forensics team out there," Reilly said, "which means there's probably a good amount of evidence still left, but that doesn't justify your actions."

"I know," Tara said, dropping her head. "I got the lecture already. Three lectures, actually. One from Marco and two from my parents."

"Make that four," I added and put my hand on her shoulder. "After our little chat tonight."

Marco continued questioning Reilly, "Why did Dr. Allen move the body from the shed?"

"He got spooked after the police showed up to do a wellness check on his wife," Reilly answered. "He had to move the body hastily, and once the body was discovered, they had to come up with a new plan."

"Burn the shed," I said.

"No," Reilly told us, "Actually, they were planning on leaving the country. I still don't know why Allen came back to erase the evidence. He wouldn't say."

"I think it's because he knew I was on to him," Tara said. "I overheard him talking to Eileen. He knew I was trying to get into the shed."

"How did he know?" I asked.

Tara dropped her head again. "I don't know."

"Wait a minute, Tara," I said. "How *did* you get into the shed?"

"The door was open," she answered.

"Tara."

She looked at me with wide eyes and then motioned to Sergeant Reilly. "I'll tell you later."

I stood up. "Let's go into the other room. I think it's time for your fourth lecture."

Once the story broke, I was getting phone calls all night. I heard from both of my brothers, aunts, cousins, friends, and some of our regular clients. At dinner, Marco told me that four different people had called to request the services of the Salvare Detective Agency.

"Marco, Christmas is coming up and that's a busy time for me. And now we're going to have more private eye work than I can handle. We'll also have to squeeze time in for Seedy and Smoke – and my parents. You'll need to print out a schedule . . ."

"Whoa, Sunshine. Aren't you being a bit too controlling?" He came around the table and picked up my hands. "There's no need to worry about that just yet. Here's an idea. Let's board the animals and take a four-day vacation to Key West."

I stared at him in shock. Was he being serious?

"Abby, we've been working so hard, we haven't taken any time for each other. So, before the craziness sets in, how about it? Will you come away with me?"

I squeezed his hands playfully. "Marco, aren't you being a little impulsive?"

"Yes." He touched the tip of my nose. "Adorably impulsive."

Flower Shop Mystery Series

MUM'S THE WORD
SLAY IT WITH FLOWERS
DEARLY DEPOTTED
SNIPPED IN THE BUD
ACTS OF VIOLETS
A ROSE FROM THE DEAD
SHOOTS TO KILL
EVIL IN CARNATIONS
SLEEPING WITH ANEMONE
DIRTY ROTTEN TENDRILS
NIGHT OF THE LIVING DANDELION
TO CATCH A LEAF
NIGHTSHADE ON ELM STREET
SEED NO EVIL
THROW IN THE TROWEL
A ROOT AWAKENING
FLORIST GRUMP
MOSS HYSTERIA
YEWS WITH CAUTION
MISSING UNDER THE MISTLETOE – Christmas Novella
TULIPS TOO LATE – Spring Novella
A FROND IN NEED – Fall Novella

Goddess of Greene St. Mysteries

STATUE OF LIMITATIONS
A BIG FAT GREEK MURDER

Continue reading for chapter one –
MISSING UNDER THE MISTLETOE
A Flower Shop Mystery Christmas Novella

MISSING UNDER THE MISTLETOE

A Flower Shop Mystery Christmas Novella

CHAPTER ONE

Bloomers Flower Shop
December 24th
9:30 am

"Abby," I heard Lottie call, trying her best to maintain a cheerful tone, "could you come out here for a minute? We have customers waiting."

I poked my head through the purple curtain separating the workroom from the sales floor and saw that Bloomers was already packed. Giving me a pointed, impatient stare was Mrs. Guilford, standing in front of the register holding a long branch of mistletoe, her wallet out, with one white glove pushed back just far enough to check her gold and diamond-laced wristwatch.

Meanwhile, Lottie, my long-time assistant, was bouncing between two couples with her hands full. Literally. She had a potted poinsettia in one hand and a white lily gift basket in the other. I immediately stopped what I was doing and headed for the register.

Normally I enjoyed the Christmas Eve morning rush, but the spindle in the workroom was still half-full of orders that needed to be finished before the store closed at four o'clock, Lottie was besieged by customers needing help in selecting gifts, Grace was attending to thirsty customers in the coffee-and-tea parlor, and Rosa hadn't yet returned from an early morning delivery. That left me popping back and forth between the workroom and shop floor trying to be everywhere at once. My head was spinning.

As I passed the parlor, I paused at the wide, arched doorway to ask Grace if she had a moment to spare, but she lifted her hands to show me a silver teapot and a plate of piping hot scones on their way to be delivered. "I wish I had time to help you out, love, but as you can see, we're jammed."

Scones. My mouth watered at the sight of Grace's homemade scones, today's flavor -blueberry pecan. I knew I should have had Rosa make her famous egg dish, *huevos ranchero,* before sending her out for that delivery. I'd hurried out of the house without having a bite since the shops around the square opened early on the morning before Christmas. Now I was starving, as I was sure my employees were. But the holidays were always crazy at Bloomers Flower Shop, so I just had to suck it up.

Where was I? Oh, yeah. *Breakfast.*

"Excuse me, Ms. Knight, but would you hurry, please?" Mrs. Guilford asked. "I am a very busy woman."

Oh, right. Mrs. Guilford.

I pushed a lock of my bright red hair out of my eyes. I'd barely had time to blow it into its usual long bob that morning and one side was hanging in my eyes and driving me crazy. "It's Abby Knight *Salvare,* now. And of course, I'll hurry. I'm so sorry you had to wait."

Rosa suddenly burst into Bloomers accompanied by a blast of cold air, causing the jingle bells we'd hung above the door to unharmoniously crash into the ceiling, stopping the store's bustle momentarily. Before scurrying past, she caught my eye, nodding her head toward the backroom, flailing the curtain behind her, leaving me standing awkwardly before my perplexed customer.

"I don't have time for this." And with that, Mrs. Guilford placed a twenty-dollar bill onto the counter. Picking up her mistletoe, she added, "Keep the change," then exited the shop in a rush.

Lottie, who had returned to the register to ring up one of her customers, leaned close to whisper, "Actually, the mistletoe was twenty-*one* dollars."

As I headed toward the workroom, I thought back to earlier that morning when Grace, Rosa, Lottie, and I had taken a brisk, enchanting stroll around New Chapel's town square. We'd left just as the sun was peeking above the two and three-story nineteenth-century buildings, to catch a glimpse of the Christmas Eve preparations already underway.

From Bloomers, we'd taken the long way around the courthouse lawn, where booths were being constructed for vendors selling leftover holiday decorations, ornaments, knit-wear, snacks, and hot apple cider later that evening. On the other side of the courthouse stood Churchill's department store, the main Christmas shopping destination of downtown New Chapel, Indiana. The large, beautifully decorated old building occupied half a city block and was central to the annual Christmas Eve celebration.

After making a full circle around the square, we stopped to inspect our booth, just across the street from Bloomers, where we'd be selling arrangements of holly, mistletoe, and poinsettias. And that reminded me – I had to stop day-dreaming and get moving. Bloomers had been hired by Churchill's to deliver and display two dozen poinsettias before the store opened at ten o'clock that morning. I glanced at my watch. We only had twenty minutes.

When I entered the workroom, I found Rosa pacing back and forth, muttering something in Spanish as she fixed the black and gold headwrap that covered her ears. Poor Rosa. It was her first year working for Bloomers and she wasn't accustomed to the holiday hassles.

"Rosa, you've got to chill out and tell me what's wrong."

"First, I am more than chilled. I am frozen stiff. I spent the last half hour standing on a small stool, hanging holly from the eaves of a Spanish colonial house, taking orders from a woman who seemed to think I knew only two words of English. *Here*...and *there!*

"And second, we have two dozen poinsettias and stands that still have to be delivered, carried inside, and arranged at Santa's Village before ten. How will we finish it all?"

"It's okay, Rosa. We can be a little late."

"Ha! I used to work for Mr. Churchill and I will tell you this, he might look like *San Nicolás* but he is no saint. He does not tolerate his employees being late. Now, where are the poinsettias so I can start loading them? I have the delivery van waiting in the alley."

"You can't load them until the stands are inside the van. I'll have to give you a hand, though, because they're heavy."

"You do not have time for that and everyone else is too busy." She started for the cooler only to pause and glance back at me, one eyebrow cocked. "Unless you want to call Marco for help, as I suggested earlier."

"We don't need Marco." Which wasn't the truth, because the stands we used were made of heavy wrought iron so they wouldn't be easily tipped over by children waiting to see Santa. But I couldn't tell Rosa that because Marco and I hadn't parted on the best of terms that morning. "Grace and Lottie will just have to manage without me for a while."

I was about to follow Rosa to the cooler when a small Christmas miracle happened. I couldn't believe I was using those words to describe my zany cousin, but when the purple curtain parted, there stood the tall, beautiful Jillian Knight Osborne with a teacup in hand, dressed almost head to toe in white.

She had on a white snow cap over her long copper-colored hair, a white turtle-neck sweater beneath a furry white vest, sparkly silver leggings, and bright white snow boots that looked like they had never even seen the snow.

Her smile turned to surprise as I rushed to hug her. "Jillian, thank God you're here! I need you out on the sales floor now."

She blinked back a sudden rush of tears. "You actually want my help?"

"Yes, so yank off that vest, grab one of the yellow smocks hanging in the storage closet, and get behind the register. That'll give Lottie a chance to catch up back here. You'll be fine."

She began listing off the reasons why she wouldn't be fine as I made my way back to the workroom. Rosa was inside one of our walk-in coolers, straining as she tried to drag two of the heavy wrought iron stands through the door.

"Rosa, you're going to hurt your back. We'll have to lift them together. Maybe take one out at a time."

"Twenty-four stands and then twenty-four poinsettias one by one? I'm telling you, Abby, we need Marco's help."

"No, we don't. We can do this if we work together." The heavy stand was stacked on top of another. We lifted them together toward the back door, then stopped. My arms were already burning.

Rosa put her hands on her hips and gave me a perplexed look. "I don't know what is going on between you and your husband, but you need to put that aside because we need his help now. Go down to his bar and get Marco or I will."

"I'm telling you we can do this, Rosa. Just bend your knees, get a good grip, and lift on the count of three. Ready? One. Two –"

It was almost ten o'clock when I knocked on the front door of Down the Hatch, Marco's bar, just two buildings down from my shop. The lights were off and there was no sign of activity, but I knew he was in there; we'd driven downtown together. I just didn't know what kind of mood I'd find him in.

"It looks like the Grinch's lair in there," Rosa said, peering into the darkened glass between her gloved hands.

"Tell me about it," I said and knocked again. As I waited for him to open the door, I glanced around. The entire square sparkled with brilliant red, green and gold decorations, shop windows abounded with Christmas candles, awnings were decorated with dangling doves, and red-wrapped wreaths hung from the fronts of doors. Then there was Marco's bar. The black hole of Christmas cheer.

Rosa turned to me and asked the question that I knew had been on everyone's mind. "What happened between you and Marco? You haven't been yourself all morning."

I sighed, feeling the start of tears. "Same thing that happened last year."

"What happened last year?"

"All I can tell you is that for some reason Marco and Christmas don't get along. I made the mistake of asking him why, but he wouldn't answer." I wiped away a stray tear. "I don't know how to reach him."

She pounded on the door, trying to get his attention. "Maybe he will tell me why."

Good luck with that, I thought.

"Morning, ladies," Marco greeted from behind us as if our earlier disagreement had never taken place. He was holding a paper coffee cup, steaming in the cold morning air.

"Marco, you must come help us," Rosa said. "*Vamonos!*"

"What's going on?"

"We have twenty-four iron stands and twenty-four pots of poinsettias to deliver and we are already late," Rosa explained. "We need your help."

He wiggled his key into the front door with his free hand. "No problem," he said casually. "Where exactly are we delivering them?"

"Santa's Village at Churchill's," Rosa answered, and instantly Marco's body tensed.

"We must be quick," Rosa continued. "Bring your coffee and come. We are late already."

"Nope. Sorry." He opened the door and stepped inside, dropping his keys onto the long, polished wood bar that filled the left side of the room. "I'm not going anywhere near that place."

"Why?" Rosa asked as we followed him into the darkened bar.

"Because I can't, that's why."

"That is not a reason," Rosa said.

"Rosa, let's go," I said.

"You want to know my reason?" Marco asked. "The Christmas carols, the shopping, the needy kids, the pushy parents. . ." He stopped and let out a long, frustrated sigh, running his fingers through the sides of his hair. "It's too much for me, that's all."

"But that is *Christmas,*" Rosa said with a puzzled frown.

"You can have it," Marco muttered.

"In other words," I said to Rosa, "bah, humbug."

Marco stopped to take a drink of his coffee. "If you want to put it that way," he said, "yes. Bah, humbug."

"Okay, I get that you don't like Christmas," Rosa said, "but think of it this way. All we need is twenty minutes to make a delivery. Maybe thirty, but you do not have to step inside the building."

Marco stood there sipping his coffee, unwavering in his decision, his behavior so unlike my handsome hero that he felt like a stranger to me.

"Forget it, Rosa," I said, giving him a scowl. "We'll manage by ourselves."

"*Santa Madre de Dios,*" Rosa cried, finally losing her patience. "What is wrong with a man who would not want to help his own wife?"

He grabbed his keys from the bar and started toward the door. "Let's get this over with."

About The Author

Kate Collins is the author of the best-selling Flower Shop Mystery series. Her books have made the New York Times Bestseller list, the Barnes & Noble mass market mystery best-sellers' lists, the Independent Booksellers' best-seller's lists, as well as booksellers' lists in the U.K. and Australia. The first three books in the FSM series are now available on audiobook. Kate's new series, GODDESS OF GREENE ST. MYSTERIES, arrived in 2019. STATUE OF LIMITATIONS is the first book in the series, with the second book, A BIG FAT GREEK MURDER, available December 2020, and a third book in the works.

In January of 2016, Hallmark Movies & Mysteries channel aired the first Flower Shop Mystery series movie, MUM'S THE WORD, followed by SLAY IT WITH FLOWERS and DEARLY DEPOTTED. The movies star Brooke Shields, Brennan Elliott, Beau Bridges and Kate Drummond.

Kate started her career writing children's stories for magazines and eventually published historical romantic suspense novels under the pen name Linda Eberhardt and Linda O'Brien. Seven romance novels later, she switched to her true love, mysteries.